MRS. MALORY AND THE LILIES THAT FESTER

A Sheila Malory Mystery

Hazel Holt

A SIGNET BOOK

SIGNET
Published by New American Library, a division of
Penguin Putnam Inc., 375 Hudson Street,
New York, New York 10014, U.S.A.
Penguin Books Ltd, 27 Wrights Lane,
London W8 5TZ, England
Penguin Books Australia Ltd, Ringwood,
Victoria, Australia
Penguin Books Canada Ltd, 10 Alcorn Avenue,
Toronto, Ontario, Canada M4V 3B2
Penguin Books (N.Z.) Ltd, 182–190 Wairau Road,
Auckland 10, New Zealand

Penguin Books Ltd, Registered Offices:
Harmondsworth, Middlesex, England

First published by Signet, an imprint of New American Library,
a division of Penguin Putnam Inc.

First Printing, June 2001
10 9 8 7 6 5 4 3 2 1

But if that flower with base infection meet,
The basest weed outbraves his dignity:
For sweetest things turn sourest by their deeds;
Lilies that fester smell far worse than weeds.

—William Shakespeare: Sonnet 94

Chapter One

"Are you *sure* you don't mind?" Rosemary asked.

"No, of course not," I said.

"Only I've got this wretched cold and even if I felt well enough to go myself I wouldn't want to give it to *her*."

"No, really, it's fine."

"And Jilly and Roger are away and Jack has this meeting of the CPRE . . ."

"Rosemary," I said, "it's all right. I don't mind in the least. I was going myself anyway."

"Even so," Rosemary said, "it's a lot to ask. I mean, Mother can be very difficult . . ."

I laughed. "I've known your mother for over fifty years now. I think I know what to expect."

"Well, I don't want her to spoil your evening. It sounds rather nice, actually. I'm rather cross I can't go. Mother hasn't missed an Antiquarians do in years. Oh well," she added hopefully, "once you're there you can off-load her onto one of her cronies."

"It'll be fine."

"She wanted to go on the coach with the others

but she does find it a bit difficult to get up the steps now."

"I usually go by car," I said, "so that I don't have to stay to the bitter end. These things do tend to go on a bit."

The Antiquarian Society is one of the more elitist groups in Taviscombe—you practically have to have your name down from birth to get into it. Peter and I were never members, but, when he died, various kind people, determined that I should be Taken Out of Myself and Given an Interest, somehow had me made a member. I must say, I quite enjoy the outings. These consist of visits to various local manor houses and minor stately homes, not normally open to the public. It is this exclusivity, of course, that makes them so desirable to people, especially to Rosemary's mother, Mrs. Dudley. As you might expect, the members of the Society are mostly retired people who like old houses and antique furniture, but who also like having a good look round other people's homes, especially rather grand ones. I have often noticed that the silver-framed photographs of the family and the laid-aside modern novel are often subjected to a closer scrutiny than the fine Chippendale table they are resting on. The evening visits are rounded off by refreshments usually taken at some carefully selected pub on the way home or, just occasionally, the owner of the house in question will lay on a buffet and make a small charge, which is donated to a local charity. It was to be one such occasion this evening, which made Mrs. Dudley more than ever determined not to miss it.

The house, Hawkcombe Manor, is a fine Tudor building, beautifully maintained by its new owner, William Bradwell, who, having made a fortune in ceramic tiles, was able to fulfill a lifelong ambition to be a country squire.

"It's tragic, really," Mrs. Dudley said as we drove through the early evening sunshine. "To think that the Southwells had to sell. I believe they're living in Torquay now, quite dreadful! Lady Millicent Southwell—she was a Ramsay, you know, before her marriage—used to come to the W.I. group meetings, and sometimes we all met at the Manor itself. *Such* a nice person she was, quite unaffected. We got along splendidly. It will be very painful to see these other people living there, but I felt I owed it to Lady Millicent to come."

The coach with the majority of the members was already drawn up at the rear of the house, and I was going to park beside it when Mrs. Dudley stopped me.

"No, Sheila. Stop just here, outside the front door."

I looked nervously at the entrance with its great studded door and the stone armorial bearings above it, but since I was more in awe of Mrs. Dudley than of the owner I obeyed meekly.

Fortunately at this moment Mervyn Gray, the secretary of the Antiquarians, came round the side of the house and took charge of Mrs. Dudley so that I was able to move the car to a less conspicu-

ous position. I found the rest of the group in the
rear courtyard admiring a couple of ornate Jacobean lead cisterns and I was relieved to see that
Mrs. Dudley had appropriated Mervyn to be her
escort and was no longer in need of my attention.
William Bradwell appeared—a large cheerful man,
happy in his good fortune and obviously delighted
to share his pleasure in his new acquisition with
anyone who was prepared to listen—and led us
into the house. There were about twenty Antiquarians, a slightly unwieldy number, so we straggled
behind him in groups and I found myself walking
with Hugh Barber and his wife, Lois. I've known
Hugh for years, he was an old friend of Peter's
and, like him, a solicitor—they'd been at the College of Law together. He was very good-looking as
a young man, tall and fair-haired and athletic, and
even now he's still extremely striking. His charming manners and warm personality mean that he
has many friends and certainly helps to account for
the substantial number of clients that have made
him a highly successful senior partner in his law
firm. I'm very fond of Hugh and was delighted to
see him. My feelings about Lois, however, are
rather mixed. She too had been something of a
beauty in her day—they had made a striking couple—but this evening she looked absolutely dreadful.

It is always extremely difficult when someone
you've always loathed is very ill. You feel sympathy, of course, but that doesn't stop you disliking
the traits that have offended you when the person

in question was perfectly well. Except that now you feel guilty. I never liked Lois Manning. She always seemed to me to be totally selfish, out for what she could get and quite ruthless about how she got it. What she wanted was Hugh, who was considered to be quite a considerable catch. I suppose they have been fairly happy together, though I know Hugh would have liked children. Lois never wanted them, of course, because then she wouldn't be the center of Hugh's world and the recipient of his complete attention and adoration. A few years ago, though, she contracted cancer and although she seemed to have made a good recovery, I had heard that there were now secondaries that were causing some concern and that she'd been in the hospital for some tests.

"Sheila!" Hugh greeted me with a smile and an expansive gesture. "How lovely to see you! Quite a lot of our friends are here today."

"Yes, it's a pretty good turnout," I said. "I imagine a lot of people wanted to see this particular house. It really is splendid, isn't it?" I turned to Lois. "It's nice to see you out and about again. How are you?"

She shrugged. "Not too marvelous."

Hugh broke in. "I thought this little outing might take Lois out of herself."

"Oh, for God's sake, Hugh," she said impatiently, "stop speaking about me in the third person!"

He gave a nervous little laugh. "I'm sorry, my dear." He cast his eyes around the room as if to find some object to comment on. "My goodness, that's a handsome tapestry." He moved toward the end of the room to examine it more closely and Lois said, "He's driving me mad! Fussing all the time!"

"It's only because he cares for you," I said.

"Yes, well, that's as it may be, but it's very irritating to live with." She spoke brusquely and without warmth and I found that I was feeling more sorry for Hugh than I was for her.

"There are some really beautiful things here," I said. "Did you see that superb dresser in the hall?"

"It's not a period I greatly care for," she said dismissively and I fell silent as we caught up with the others in the paneled dining room.

I was glad to move away and was speaking to some of the other members when I heard Mrs. Dudley holding forth.

"That is a very handsome Georgian coffeepot, but I think mine is even finer." She caught sight of me and called out, "Don't you agree, Sheila—that mine is a finer example?"

Heads turned to look at me, including that of the owner, William Bradwell, and I wished, as I so often did when I was with Mrs. Dudley, that the earth would open and swallow me up.

"Yes," I mumbled, "yours is very fine."

Hugh caught my eye and smiled sympathetically and we all moved on. The buffet was laid out in the Great Hall and was greeted with many murmurs of approval. Obviously William Bradwell was determined to make a good show and the plates of salmon mayonaise and delicious ham and cold roast beef rapidly disappeared, as did the magnificently rich sherry trifle. The wine circulated freely and the whole atmosphere soon became very relaxed indeed. When I had fulfilled my duty by Mrs. Dudley ("Just a couple of slices of the ham and some of the roast beef, please, Sheila—no, a *little* more than that . . .") and seen her safely in deep conversation with one of her fellow gossips, I found a chair and sat down beside Mrs. Beresford. Esme Beresford was a friend of my mother's, so I am always pleased to see her. She is now in her eighties but looks much younger, being tall and still very upright and with a lively manner and apparently undiminished energy.

"How nice to see you," I said. "You're looking very elegant!" And, indeed, she always did, wearing those smart but timeless clothes that only the really well-off can afford.

She smiled. "Thank you, my dear—I do my best!"

"I thought you might have gone off by now," I said. Mrs. Beresford spent some months in the South of France. "Where is it you are going this year?"

"I am going to Antibes. I went to Nice last year but I'm afraid it isn't what it was in the old days. No, Antibes is still relatively unspoilt and it has so many happy memories for me—as you know Herbert and I had a villa there for many years. I shall stay at the Hotel Royale, it is quite near the

Chateaux d'Horizon, where we used to go to Maxine Elliot's parties before the war."

I sighed. "How glamorous it all sounds!"

She smiled. "Yes, I think it was. True glamour, not this ersatz 'pop' stuff!" She put the word in palpable quotes. "I was lucky and you, Sheila, did see a little of what it was all about, but I am so sad for the young today!"

"I suppose what they've never had they won't miss," I said.

"I suppose so, but there seem to be no standards nowadays of either morals or behavior. And how *messy* they look in those dreadful clothes!" She sighed. "Oh well, I'm just an old woman who has been left over from another age."

I laughed. "I must say I often feel the same, especially when I'm watching television!"

"Still, you have Michael to keep you up to date. I would have liked children, but it was not to be."

"Actually, Michael isn't what you would call up to date, more *traditional*, you might say. Perhaps it's being a solicitor and having to wear a suit every day." Out of the corner of my eye I saw Mrs. Dudley beckoning me. "Oh, I'm so sorry I must go, I think Mrs. Dudley wants to leave now. I'm giving her a lift home. Have a marvelous time in Antibes—I shall think of you enviously when the autumn gales begin to blow!"

On the way home Mrs. Dudley, still remarkably lively in spite of the advanced hour, questioned me closely about Mrs. Beresford's movements.

"Antibes, you say? I wouldn't care for *that*. I

have never felt the need to go abroad—Taviscombe
is good enough for me. I like to be in a place where
I am *known*. In my opinion all this traveling about
is just a form of showing off." She gave a little
snort of contempt. "And besides, all sorts of people
are going abroad nowadays. You'd never know *who*
you were mixing with, even in the most expensive
places—lottery winners and people like that!"

"I wouldn't think there'd be many lottery winners in Antibes," I said. "I always imagine they'd
go to Spain or Florida. Anyway, Mrs. Beresford
wants to go back to Antibes because they used to
have a villa there before the war."

"Oh yes, Herbert Beresford was a very successful
businessman. I never really understood what his
particular line was—something not quite right, I always felt. I remember my late husband saying once
that he was lucky not to have been wiped out—I
think that was the phrase—by something or other.
Anyway, *rather* suspicious. He died just after the
war and, although I don't imagine Esme Beresford
is as rich as she was—who *is* nowadays, with these
appalling taxes—she is quite comfortably off. Of
course, Hugh Barber handles her affairs, has done
for years. I expect she'll have left him something
quite substantial in her will, since there are no children . . ."

She returned to the subject of Herbert Beresford's
possible business interests and I abstracted my
mind—as I frequently do in Mrs. Dudley's company—and concentrated on driving through the
dark lanes, avoiding the transfixed rabbits caught

in the glare of the headlights and other such hazards of nocturnal rural driving.

I don't believe she drew breath from the moment we left Hawkcombe Manor until I finally delivered her to her door and into the capable hands of her slave, Elsie, who had waited up for her. I was quite exhausted and reflected, not for the first time, that an evening spent in Mrs. Dudley's company took far more out of me than the most strenuous physical exercise.

Chapter Two

"Guess what, Ma?" Michael said as he slung his cricket bag onto the work top, to the imminent danger of a dish of stewed plums I had left there to cool. "Guess who's come back to Taviscombe?"

"Who?"

"Thea Wyatt."

"How lovely! Have you seen her?"

"Yes, I ran into her in the bank this morning. She's going to work with Hugh Barber's firm—assistant solicitor."

"Well, I *am* pleased."

"Good, because I've invited her to supper on Wednesday. Is that all right?"

"I don't think I've anything on. I'll look at the calendar. But, yes, it will be so nice to see her again."

"Great." Michael began to pull garments from his bag and stuff them into the washing machine. "Do you think you could do something about a cricket shirt for Saturday?" he enquired hopefully.

"He looked really pleased," I said to Rosemary, when I went round there later to report on the Antiquarians evening. "He's always had a bit of a thing about her and he was quite upset when she went to London."

"Oh yes, I remember. She went away when her father married again, didn't she?"

"That's right. That awful woman, Glynis, made life really miserable for her. Philip never saw it—I suppose he didn't want to—and so Thea thought it would be better if she went right away. She was very upset when her mother died in that car accident—Sara Wyatt was such a nice person. Do you remember her at school? She was a few years younger than us."

"A pretty girl with long fair plaits? Played tennis rather well?"

"That's right."

"And Thea's come back?"

"Yes. Philip's retired now and they've moved to Wales—Glynis came from Swansea or somewhere. And apparently Thea didn't really like London and always wanted to come back here."

"And she's going to work for Hugh Barber's firm?"

"Yes, it was really lucky that there was a vacancy there. I'm glad she's a solicitor, too; it means that she and Michael have a lot in common."

Rosemary laughed. "Are you by any chance wearing your matchmaker's hat?" she asked.

"No," I protested. "It's just that I've always liked Thea and—oh, well, perhaps I am a bit. But Michael is thirty now and he really ought to be thinking about settling down."

"And you want some grandchildren?"

"Of course I do! Anyway, nothing may come of it, but, as I said, she's a really nice girl and I shall look forward to seeing her again."

Thea seemed really pleased to be invited to supper.

"It's *so* lovely to see old friends again," she said, stooping to pat Tris, who had greeted her in the hall. "I've really missed Taviscombe and all the people I used to know. Oh, look! He's brought his ball for me to throw!"

"You're very honored," I said. "He doesn't do that for everyone."

She laughed and threw the ball and Tris retrieved it and brought it back to her.

"Where's the other one?" she asked. "You used to have a spaniel, too, didn't you?"

"Tess? Yes. I'm afraid she died last month. She was fourteen, which is a very good age for a spaniel."

"Oh, I'm sorry. You must miss her."

"Yes, we do. Tris most of all, of course. It's funny though, he and Foss—that's our Siamese, do you remember him?—have suddenly become much closer. They even sleep in the same basket now, which is something they'd never dream of doing before."

"I suppose when someone dies it's natural to cling to those we have left. But," she added sadly, "sometimes they don't want us to cling to them."

"You mean your father," I said tentatively.

"Yes. I thought that we would just go on to-gether. It didn't occur to me that that might not be enough for him. I suppose it was selfish of me."

"Glynis Williams was a really scheming sort of person," I said vehemently. "She knew a good thing when she saw one and went right after it. Once she'd got her eye on him, your father never stood a chance. He had too nice a nature to see what was happening!"

Thea smiled ruefully. "I'm afraid you're right. Still," she said, "he seems perfectly happy so I must be glad it's all turned out so well for him."

"And we're all glad," I said warmly, "that you're back in Taviscombe."

"It's lovely to be back. I somehow never felt *right* in London. I mean, it's marvelous for a visit, but I knew I didn't want to live there."

"You had a very good job," Michael said. "Farley and Grainger are top pensions lawyers. The money must have been terrific!"

"Yes it was, and I know I could have made a great deal if I'd stayed, but, honestly, it occurred to me that if I *did* make a lot of money I'd only spend it on a country cottage that I'd never have time to visit! I don't think I'm a city sort of person. Any-way," she said, turning to Michael, "you're not one to talk. Didn't you turn down a super job in Lon-don to stay in Taviscombe?"

He laughed. "True. Oh well, let's agree that we are the sensible ones."

"Are you enjoying working for Barber and Free-man?" I asked.

"Oh, yes. Mr. Barber is really helpful and kind and the others seem to be very nice." She hesitated slightly. "Though I must confess I'm not too keen on Gordon Masefield."

"Ah," Michael said. "Ghastly Gordon. He's a bit of a pain."

"In what way?" I asked.

"Oh, very full of himself, thinks he knows everything. Drives a flashy car he can't really afford and thinks he's God's gift to women."

"I thought he was married," I said. "Didn't he marry that nice little Wendy Lewis? I seem to remember seeing a picture in the *Free Press* a while back."

"Yes, he did, and there's a little girl, but that doesn't seem to stop him."

"Oh dear."

"Actually, I'm not entirely sure that he'll be staying with Barber and Freeman," Michael said to Thea, "so you may not have to put up with him for much longer. Hugh was hinting that he might have to get rid of him—something not quite right with the way he dealt with one of his clients, I gather, though of course Hugh was careful not to say too much."

"Well, I can't say I'd be sorry," Thea said, "because everything else is so good there."

"How is your flat?" I asked. "Are you properly settled in now? Is there anything we can do to help? Michael is very good at putting up shelves."

"It's fine. I'm pretty well straight now. Mind you, I wouldn't say no to a few more shelves. My books seem to have been breeding while they've been in storage—I'm sure there's twice as many as I had before!"

"Any time," Michael said. "Just say the word."

The door was suddenly pushed open and Foss came bustling in and made straight for Thea and jumped onto her lap.

"Oh, do put him down," I said. "He'll ruin your skirt—he's a devil for pulling threads and he'll cover you with hairs!"

"He's fine," Thea said, stroking him. "He's a beautiful boy!"

I got up. "I'll just go and see about supper. Don't let him be a nuisance."

"She really is *so* nice," I reported back to Rosemary, "and she was sweet with the animals."

"Oh, well then!"

I laughed. "Yes, well. But she's so easy and comfortable—someone I can *chat* to. Not all that common among the young nowadays. What my mother used to call an old-fashioned girl."

"I know what you mean. It can be really difficult—some of them seem to be talking a totally different language. So you think Michael might be interested?"

"I think so. He's going to put up some shelves for her."

"That's a good sign. And what about Thea? How do you think she feels?"

"I don't know, really. She's a naturally friendly girl, so it's hard to tell. One thing—from what I could gather, I don't think she's involved with anyone in London, so that's a good thing! Anyway, she's going to watch Michael play cricket on Saturday, which argues a nice nature if nothing else!"

"Oh, good. I'll probably see her there, then. I promised Jack I'd help with the teas."

Saturday was fine and warm—well, at least there was no rain and the wind had dropped—and it was not unpleasant to sit outside the pavilion on one of the wooden benches there. From past experience I avoided the canvas chairs and I had remembered to bring a couple of cushions with me.

Thea arrived quite early, looking fresh and cool in a cornflower blue dress that set off her fair hair.

"Come and sit here," I invited. "I brought a spare cushion for you."

"Oh, lovely." She sat down and looked about her. "Isn't this nice! Just the sort of thing I've missed in London!"

Rosemary came out of the pavilion and sat beside us.

"I mustn't stay long," she said. "Anthea's just setting up the tea urn for me—I can never manage it. It always makes terrifying hissing noises and frightens me to death! It's so nice to see you back in Taviscombe, Thea."

"It's lovely to be back. I've missed it very much."

"Sheila says you've got a flat on West Hill."

"Yes. I was very lucky. Hugh knew of one that was just coming onto the market, really nice with a marvelous view of the sea from the sitting-room window. Hugh did ask me to stay with them for a bit while I was looking around, but Lois wasn't very well so I didn't feel I could, but it was very nice of him to offer."

"I thought she looked quite dreadful," I said, "when I saw them at that Antiquarians thing."

"I think Hugh's very worried about her," Thea said.

"She's always been very demanding," Rosemary said, "and I should think it's even worse now."

"It is," I agreed. "Michael said Hugh's had to give up the boat because she said it took up too much of his time, and you know how passionately he loved it!"

"I know. He used to make all his young assistant solicitors crew for him. At least you've escaped that, Thea!"

Thea laughed. "Oh, I would have loved it. I used to sail with my father."

Rosemary got to her feet. "I'd better go or Anthea will have made a martyr of herself by cutting all the sandwiches. You must come and have supper, Thea, when Jilly and her husband are back."

"When does Roger's thing finish?" I asked.

"In about three weeks, I think, and then they're going to stay with some friends in Florida and take the children to Disney World."

"Rosemary's son-in-law, Roger, is a chief inspector," I explained to Thea, "and he's over in America on some sort of police exchange thing."

"He was able to take Jilly and the children with

him," Rosemary said, "which is lovely for them, but I do miss the children. I shall hardly recognize them when they get back!" She glanced back at the pavilion. "Oh dear, the teams are coming out. I'd better go. See you soon."

Taviscombe won the toss and Michael came out to open the batting with his friend Jonah. I know he was worried about this because he usually batted lower down the order but Jonah, who is the captain, for some technical reason I didn't understand, said he wanted to try him out as an opener. I explained all this to Thea and she smiled. "I think you're as nervous as he is!"

"I think I am."

Still, Michael settled in and started to make some runs.

"Oh, lovely shot!" Thea applauded a really nice cover drive. "He's doing splendidly!"

I suppose most mothers are nervous when their offspring are performing in any way—it was the same when he was in the school play, I could hardly bear to watch—and Rosemary, whose son Martin is a history don at a Scottish university, says that even now she gets into a dreadful state when she goes to one of his lectures. Still, I began to relax a little and enjoy it.

Jonah was out to a ferocious yorker and the next man gave an easy catch to first slip, then Gordon Masefield came in. He looked around the field with a slightly contemptuous air, prodded the pitch with his bat and faced up to the bowling. He was, I must admit, a good attacking batsman, but selfishly determined to keep the batting, taking a single at the end of an over when there were two perfectly good runs there. I could see that Michael was getting impatient with him and I was pleased to see that when he managed to keep the bowling he hit a couple of really good boundaries. But what should have been a team effort was rapidly degenerating into a contest between two players on the same side.

"That awful man!" Thea exclaimed indignantly. "He's ruining everything, just to show off."

"I'm afraid Michael's lost his temper," I said. "They seem to be having a sort of duel out there!"

"Well, you can't blame Michael," Thea said. "He's been provoked beyond measure!"

Just then Gordon Masefield hit a ball toward square leg and called for a run. The fielder was already moving toward the ball and Michael hesitated just a moment too long before he set off and was run out.

"Oh, no!" Thea cried. "That was so unfair. It was perfectly obvious there wasn't a run there! I'm sure Gordon did that deliberately to get Michael out."

Michael walked slowly off the field, his lips compressed in a thin line and very red in the face and I saw that he was trying hard to control his anger. He disappeared into the pavilion and I said, "Poor love, he'll be very disappointed."

"He could have made a century, if that hateful creature hadn't behaved so badly," Thea said.

I smiled slightly at her vehemence and thought

that her sympathy might very well go a long way to consoling Michael for the loss of his wicket.

When he emerged from the pavilion and came and sat beside us, I was glad to see that he had recovered his temper and was his usual cheerful self.

"Oh well," he said, sitting down on the bench beside Thea, "it's only a game."

"But it wasn't *fair*!" Thea said. "That was a really rotten thing to do."

"It doesn't do to take it all too seriously," Michael said. "We all know what Gordon's like—he always has to be seen to be the best at everything."

"But that's not the point," Thea said heatedly.

I got up and handed my cushion to Michael.

"I just want to have a word with Rosemary," I said and moved away, leaving Michael to bask in the healing warmth of Thea's indignation.

Chapter Three

The following Monday I was passing the offices of Barber and Freeman in the Avenue when a figure I knew came out.

"Hello, Eileen," I said. "How are you? I haven't seen you for ages!"

Eileen Newton used to be Peter's secretary and it was he who encouraged her to take the exams which led to her becoming a legal executive, which was the post she held now.

"Oh, Mrs. Malory, how nice to see you!"

"Is this your lunch hour? I was just going to have a sandwich and a cup of coffee in the Buttery. Won't you join me?"

She hesitated for a moment. "Well, I do have to go up to the surgery with Father's prescription . . ."

"You can do that afterward," I said. "It can be a very quick sandwich!"

Her long, rather sad face lightened with a smile and she said, "Yes, yes, thank you. That would be very nice."

Since it was only just after twelve o'clock, the Buttery wasn't too crowded and we were able to find a table at the back, where it was quiet and we could talk in peace.

"Well now," I said when the problem of what sort of sandwich had been settled, "how is your father?"

Old Mr. Newton had had a stroke and, although he'd recovered his powers of speech, he was still confined to a wheelchair. Eileen's mother died some years ago, so the whole burden of nursing had fallen on her shoulders.

"Father's much the same, I'm afraid, and Dr. Macdonald doesn't hold out much hope of him getting any better. He's still having physio, but at his age it really isn't helping a great deal."

"I'm so sorry. It must be very difficult for you being out at work all day. How are you coping?"

"Well, the district nurse comes in several times a week and he has meals-on-wheels, which is a great help."

"It's still a lot of work for you."

"Oh, Father's very cheerful—you know how he is. And I was able to get away at Easter to stay with my cousin Kathleen in Illfracombe. Father had a week in West Lodge. It's very nice there—pricey, but it's worth it."

"I'm so glad you had a little break. It does make such a difference if you can get right away." I put a sweetener in my coffee and stirred it. "So how are you liking it at Barber and Freeman?"

She hesitated a moment before answering and I had the impression that she was feeling carefully for the right words. "Oh, it's a wonderful opportunity. I was most grateful to Mr. Barber for taking me on."

"I'm sure he was very glad to have you, Eileen. Peter always said how good you were and how much he relied on you."

"Mr. Malory was a lovely person to work for. I'll never forget how wonderful he was when Mother died."

"I'm sure Mr. Barber is a good person to work for, too."

"Oh yes, he's always very kind and thoughtful. And he has such a lot on his mind at the moment."

"Of course, poor Lois. I saw her the other day and I was really shocked at how ill she looked."

"She's very poorly. I believe"—here Eileen lowered her voice as people do when they are talking about serious illness—"the doctors have only given her about six months."

"How dreadful!"

"Well, that's what Nurse Clayden told Father when she came in to see to him the other day."

"Poor Lois. And poor Hugh. I can't imagine how he will go on without her."

"He's taking her on a cruise soon, I believe," Eileen said. "On the QE2."

"She's always loved cruises," I said. "As distinct from sailing on Hugh's boat—she never did like that! But all their married life he's tried to give her everything she wants and, to be honest, she's always been a very *demanding* woman. Still, I do see that he wants to make things as pleasant as possible for her."

Eileen nodded. "Well, you would, wouldn't you? I'm so sorry for him. And in spite of everything he's always so pleasant and everything."

"So you enjoy working there?"

"Oh yes," she replied emphatically. "I'm really grateful to be in such a good firm."

"Is old Mr. Freeman still there?"

"Yes, though he only comes in three days a week now. So Mr. Barber is really the senior partner and then there's Mr. Chapman, he's the other partner."

"Michael's friend Jonah is one of the assistant solicitors, of course, and now Thea Wyatt has joined you. We were so glad that she's come back to Taviscombe—we are very fond of her."

"I haven't had a lot to do with her yet, but she seems a really nice person."

"I think she's enjoying being there. She said how friendly everyone has been and how helpful. Mind you," I added, "I don't think she took to your associate solicitor, Gordon Masefield, and I can't say I blame her. From what I've seen of him he sounds really unpleasant! Oh dear, perhaps I shouldn't have said that! Since you work in the same firm!"

"No, you're absolutely right!" Eileen spoke quite vigorously. "He's a very unpleasant young man altogether." She stopped abruptly, as if she felt she had said too much. "Goodness, is that the time! I must rush if I'm going to get to the doctor's. Thank you so much for a lovely lunch, Mrs. Malory. It's been really nice having a little chat." She picked up her handbag and got to her feet.

"If you should ever feel like popping round I know Father would love to see you."

I watched her, a tall, rather gaunt figure, picking her way through the tables to the door with some sympathy. I knew from my own experience (my mother was an invalid for many years) how difficult such a situation can be. However loving the relationship, the patient always bears a tremendous burden of gratitude and the carer can't help the occasional feeling of vexation, which gives rise immediately to guilt and remorse, while a resolute brightness and cheerfulness on one side can provoke feelings of irritation in the other. It's not easy. Still, Eileen seemed to be coping quite well and at least she had the security of a good job to provide those little extras that make all the difference in such circumstances.

I mentioned her to Thea that evening. She had asked Michael and me to a meal to show us her new flat.

"Eileen Newton? Oh yes, Jackie told me about her father. It must be really awful for her. She does look quite wretched sometimes. I believe she's very good at her job—a bit slow, Jonah says, but very conscientious. I haven't had much to do with her so far but she seems very nice and helpful. So, what will you have to drink? Gin and tonic for you, Mrs. Malory?"

"That would be lovely, but do, please, call me Sheila."

"Thank you, I'd like that." She turned to

Michael. "And beer for you? I hope it's the right sort—I think I've seen you drinking it! Well then, what do you think of the flat? I wanted to get everything more or less sorted out before I invited anyone, so you're the first!"

It was a very pleasant flat on the higher slopes of West Hill, with a good view of the sea from the sitting-room windows.

"It's lovely," I said as I stood with a glass in my hand admiring a brilliant red and gold sunset over the bay. "And such nice big rooms."

"It was a private house, ages ago, when people lived in big houses. It used to be called 'Normandene.' Some people called Hertford lived here, I can just remember them."

"Oh yes, so they did! Elizabeth Hertford founded the Taviscombe branch of the W.I. some time in the twenties. My mother used to know her quite well. I believe they had this house built." I looked around at the elegant proportions of the room. "It's certainly very spacious."

"Lovely high ceilings," Thea said, "and lots of room for my heavy Victorian furniture!"

"It does look nice."

"It's mostly from home; it was my grandmother's. Glynis didn't like it—she only likes modern stuff, thank goodness, so when they moved to Wales Father said I could take whatever I liked. I couldn't have the bigger pieces in London because my flat was too small, so it's been in storage. It's lovely to have it about me again. I sort of feel it's happy too!" She laughed. "Is that silly?"

"No," I said firmly, "I'm sure you're absolutely right." I looked around me. "Where do you want those shelves?"

Thea indicated two alcoves on either side of the large fireplace. "I think there, don't you?" She turned to Michael. "Are you sure you don't mind?" she asked.

"No, no trouble at all. They should go in there very well. I've brought a rule with me and I'll get them measured up so that I can order the wood. Do you want polished wood or would you rather have them painted white?"

I left them to their discussion and returned to the window. The sun had almost set and was just a glimmer on the sea and far out across the Channel the lights of Wales were now visible in the gathering dusk. I looked across at Thea and Michael and thought how right they looked together, laughing over the metal rule that kept snapping shut as they tried to measure with it. I would miss Michael very much if he left home, but it was inevitable that one day he would, and I couldn't imagine he would ever find anyone nicer or more suitable than Thea.

"You're getting very Jane Austen these days," Rosemary said. "You know—it is a truth universally acknowledged and all that."

"Well, there's no fortune on either side," I replied, "but they're so *comfortable* together, if you know what I mean."

Rosemary nodded. "Yes, I do know. I felt that about Jilly and Roger straight away. And"—she

sighed—"I never felt it about Martin and Charlotte."

"No."

Rosemary had been very distressed when her
son Martin and his wife, Charlotte, were divorced a
year ago.

"Did I tell you," she asked, "that Martin may be
going to the University of Chicago for a year in Oc-
tober? Some sort of visiting fellowship."

"Oh dear, I am sorry—it's so far away!"

"Well, nowadays Chicago isn't that much farther
away than Edinburgh. We don't see that much of
him, anyway."

"Have you heard from Jilly and Roger?" I asked
to take her mind off this gloomy subject. "How are
the children enjoying America?"

Her face brightened. "Oh, they love it. Jilly says
she doesn't think she'll be able to get Alex to eat
anything but hamburgers and hot dogs ever again!
The weather's so gorgeous they live outside most
of the time and Roger takes them to the beach
every day when he gets home."

"Roger's absolutely marvelous with them. He's
so nice, you're very lucky!"

"Well, I hope you're equally lucky with Thea."

"It's really good, you know," I said thoughtfully.
"I can *relax* with her—it's almost like having a
daughter, something I always wanted!"

As the weeks went by, Thea and I continued to
get on well and sometimes went on shopping expeditions together, always a good test of compatabil-

ity. One Saturday we had gone a little further afield than usual and were combing the shops of Exeter in search of a dress for Thea.

"It's ridiculous," she said. "*Vogue* said that gray was going to be the new black, but the word doesn't seem to have reached Exeter yet! Anyway," she went on, "it doesn't look as if we're *allowed* to have dresses this year."

"I know," I said, holding up a sad-looking floor-length creation in floral cotton voile. "I mean, can you think of anything more unbecoming!"

"I should know by now," Thea said, "that it's pretty hopeless to go shopping with something definite in mind. You never find it."

"I remember one year when I longed for a red summer skirt. I looked for it all season. When eventually I did find one, exactly what I wanted, I didn't buy it because I felt by then that I'd had it and worn it all summer and was sick to death of it!"

Thea laughed. "Let's give it a rest and have some lunch."

"Good idea. There's a pub in the High Street that does rather good lunches. It's not far."

We sat for a while with our drinks looking at the menu.

"There's a blackboard over there with today's specials on it," I said. "Shall we go and see if there's anything there that we like."

"Mm. Very trendy," Thea said, studying it. "I think I'll have the brandade of salt cod, whatever that is."

"It sounds quite exotic. I'll try it too."

I gave the order to the barman and was moving away when I saw, sitting at a table in a far corner, someone I thought I recognized.

"Isn't that Gordon Masefield?" I asked Thea in a low voice.

She turned to look. "Yes, it is."

"Well that's certainly not his wife with him."

"No. It's Jackie, one of the secretaries from the office."

We sat down at our table and I said, "I don't think they saw us."

"I hope not. It would be very embarrassing."

"Well, if they do look this way you've got your back to them, and I don't expect he'd recognize me." I took a sip of my gin and tonic. "I suppose he thought they wouldn't run into anyone they knew this far away from Taviscombe. He really is a nasty piece of work."

"It's very silly of Jackie," Thea said. "I mean, she knows he's married. His wife sometimes comes into the office, to bring him files from home when he's forgotten them and things like that."

"They certainly seem very involved," I said, peering into the dimly lit corner of the bar where I could just see two heads bent close to each other.

"It's quite extraordinary," Thea said. "She's a pretty girl, I'd have thought she'd have a boyfriend of her own. I can't imagine what the attraction can be!"

"I suppose it's the older-man thing. And, of course, he probably spends quite a bit of money on her. What sort of girl is she?"

Thea shrugged. "I don't know, really. She works for Jonah, mostly. I think she's efficient at her job, though I seem to remember Jonah complaining that she wasn't in one day and saying that she probably had a hangover from too much partying."

"Just our friend Gordon's cup of tea. Poor little Wendy. I don't suppose she feels much like clubbing, or whatever it is young people do nowadays, not with a toddler to look after and probably not enough sleep!"

"Do you think she knows?"

"About Gordon's peccadillos? Probably. Even if she doesn't admit it to herself."

"Do you think I ought to tell Jonah so that he could have a word with Jackie?" Thea asked.

"Better not," I said. "Office romances are tricky things—it might lead to ill feelings all round and you've got to work with them all."

"You're probably right. Anyway, I should think Jackie's old enough to know what she's doing. Oh good, here's our food."

The brandade of cod turned out to be a sort of fishy mousse and was very delicious. By the time we'd finished it and I looked again in the lovers' direction, they had gone.

"Just as well," Thea said. "I really didn't want them to know that I'd seen them. Are you going to go back and get that cotton sweater? I think you should. That soft raspberry color really suits you."

Although I didn't mention what I'd seen to Jonah, I did sound him out about Gordon Masefield in general terms when he next came round to see Michael.

"Gordon? Yes, he is an unpleasant piece of work. I suppose you're thinking of the way he got Michael out at the match the other day. I'm very tempted not to play him again. I know he's a useful bat but he really doesn't get on at all well with the rest of the team—too much out for himself, if you know what I mean."

"But if you dropped him, wouldn't that make it awkward for you at work?" I asked.

"Yes, I suppose it might. But I'm not going to have him behaving like that again."

"Put me further down the order," Michael suggested, "back in my old place at number four. I'm really much happier there. Then Ghastly Gordon might be out before I come in."

"Well, it might work," Jonah said. "It does seem to be you that he's got his knife into, though he's not exactly affable to any of the team."

"What is he like to work with?" I asked. "Does everyone there dislike him too?"

"More or less. Of course he has brought quite a lot of work in, but he does grab whatever else is going."

"All solicitors do that," Michael observed.

"Yes, but he's more ruthless than most, and more blatant. Actually, I don't think Hugh has a very high regard for him. There was a case not long ago that turned out to be rather messy—a divorce that Gordon handled. He was acting for the wife and he really took the husband to the cleaners. I believe the poor chap tried to commit suicide. That's *not* the sort of thing that Barber and Freeman like to be mixed up in!"

"I can imagine!"

"There've been other things, too. As a matter of fact I'm surprised he's lasted so long. Though, as I said, he's got a lot of contacts and does bring in a fair amount of business, especially on the commercial side. Hugh's taken him off domestics now."

"So I should think!"

Michael broke in with some remark about the cricket team and I went out into the kitchen to make some coffee and left them to it. But I thought it was a pity that Thea had to work in the same office as such an unpleasant person as Gordon Masefield and hoped she didn't have to have much to do with him.

Chapter Four

A few days later, I was on my hands and knees trying to get a stain out of the carpet when Michael and Thea came in. Foss's overenthusiastic investigation of one of my potted plants had led to the whole thing crashing to the ground with wet earth, bits of plant, and pottery shards everywhere. Actually having potted plants at all with Foss around is a triumph of hope over experience, since he either chews the ends off the leaves or hooks the soil out of the pot with his paws.

"Oh, *there* you are," Michael said. "I didn't see you down there."

I saw at once that they had something they were bursting to tell me. I got slowly to my feet and took off my apron. I thought I knew what they were going to say and it seemed to me somehow wrong to be hearing it in an apron.

"Ma . . ." Michael began.

"She's guessed," Thea said. "Look at the way she's smiling!"

"Is it?" I asked.

"Yes," Thea said. "We're engaged. I hope you don't mind."

"*Mind!* My dear girl, I'm *delighted!*"

I hugged them both and we all started to talk at once and Tris came in and began barking because of the general air of excitement, and everything was pandemonium.

"Goodness," I said, when I finally got my breath back, "I ought to open a bottle of champagne! We still have that one that Freddy gave us for Christmas."

"Actually," Thea said, "since it's four o'clock in the afternoon, I think I'd rather have a nice cup of tea."

"Anyway," Michael said, "champagne always gives you a dreadful headache."

So we had some tea and I enquired about their plans.

"We thought a spring wedding," Thea said. "We'd rather like to enjoy being engaged for a bit."

"It's a splendidly old-fashioned thing to be," I said. "I'm so glad. What about the ring?"

"We're going into Taunton on Monday to choose one," Michael said.

"I wonder," I said hesitantly. "I wonder . . . now, Thea, this is only an idea and I want you to be completely honest with me about this . . ."

"Yes?" Thea said enquiringly.

"I don't know how you would feel about having my mother's ring. I've never worn it, it somehow didn't feel right. But I'd like you to have it anyway—I'm sure that's what she would have wanted—whether or not you want it for an engagement ring. No," I continued, "don't say anything until you've seen it. I'll go and fetch it."

I took the red velvet box from the drawer in my dressing table and gave it to Michael. He opened it and handed it to Thea.

"If you'd rather have a modern one," I said, "I shall quite understand and I promise you I won't be offended or anything."

It really is a very lovely ring. It is a large, very fine aquamarine set in diamonds and platinum. Thea gasped. "Oh, it's *beautiful!*"

"My father had it specially made for my mother when they were engaged sometime in the nineteen-twenties."

"May I really have it?"

"Of course! I'm so pleased that you like it!"

Michael put the ring on her finger. "All right?" he asked.

"Wonderful!"

"Jolly good," he said. "Think of the money we've saved!"

"Michael!"

"Only joking." He turned to me. "Thank you, Ma. That was a good thought."

"Can I tell people?" I asked.

Michael laughed. "I fully expect you to be on the phone to Rosemary before we're out of the door," he said.

Rosemary, of course, was delighted with the news.

"You've been maneuvering for this ever since Thea came back to Taviscombe!" she said.

"Not maneuvering," I protested. "But I certainly hoped it might happen."

"You're going to miss him." Rosemary looked at me anxiously.

"Yes," I said, "I will. Actually when the euphoria died down I did feel a little pang, but it's so very much what I want for him. Besides, they'll still be in Taviscombe. I'm very lucky."

"Where are they going to live?"

"They'll move into Thea's flat to begin with—it's quite spacious—and then look for a house as and when."

"And what about the wedding?"

"At St. James's, sometime in May, they think. I don't think Philip and Glynis will do much of the arranging. I mean, even if they were still in Taviscombe, I don't see Glynis being very helpful, do you? No, Thea will see to things herself and she's asked me if I'll help."

"Which, of course, pleased you no end?"

"Of course! No, really, Rosemary, it's all so marvelous. We're all so lucky, I feel I ought to keep my fingers permanently crossed!"

"Well, I'm really pleased for you all. Tell them I want first look at the wedding present list!"

A few weeks later I was in the front garden deadheading the geraniums. Because the sun was hot Tris stayed in the house, but Foss was lying on the porch, apparently somnolent but occasionally bat-

ting with his paw at any insect rash enough to
come within reach. I was just about to go and get a
trowel to loosen the soil in the planters when, to
my surprise, Thea's car turned into the drive. I
went forward to meet her just as Thea stumbled
out and, leaving the car door open, rushed toward
me. I could see at once that something was seriously wrong. Normally so neat, she looked dishev-
elled, her face was streaked with tears, and when
she spoke the words tumbled out wildly, not making any sense.

"I'm so sorry . . . I didn't know what to do . . . I
had to get away . . . it was so horrible!"

I put my arm round her and led her into the
house. "It's all right," I said. "Take it gently. Come
into the house and sit down."

I sat her beside me on the sofa and took one of
her hands. She was shaking and for a while she
seemed unable to say anything. I got up and went
over to the sideboard and poured a little brandy
into a glass and made her drink it. After a time she
seemed calmer and I said, "Now then, tell me what
has happened."

She drew a deep breath and shook her head as if
to clear it.

"I'm so sorry," she repeated, "so sorry to come to
you like this."

"My dear girl, don't be silly. Of course you must
come to me if there's something wrong. Can you
tell me about it?"

She made a great effort and seemed to pull herself together. "Yes," she said, "I'll tell you." Her

voice was steadier now and she spoke quickly, as if
to get the story over and done with. "I had to go
into Gordon Masefield's office to ask him about
one of the clients. He started to chat me up. He'd
tried it once before but I'd turned it off with a
joke—well, we have to work together and I
thought it would be embarrassing to have a row
about it. This time he was more persistent, so I told
him about the engagement. Then he made some
horrible remarks about Michael—he really does
seem to dislike him—and I lost my temper. This
seemed to amuse him for some reason, I suppose
there are men who are turned on by that sort of
thing, because he got up and made a grab at me. I
must have acted instinctively, because the next
thing I knew he was on the floor. I'm almost as tall
as he is and quite strong, so I must have given him
a pretty violent push. The thing is . . ." She hesitated. "The thing is, when I looked down at him his
head was bleeding and he was unconscious. He
must have caught his head on the corner of the
desk when he fell down."

"Oh, my dear! You must have felt awful!"

She nodded gratefully. "It was horrible. I didn't
know what to do. I was so shaken, I just stood
there stupidly looking down at him. I thought I'd
killed him! That moment seemed to last forever,
but then, thank God, I heard a groan and I saw that
he'd come round. At first I don't think he knew
what had happened and then he saw me. Sheila,
I've never seen anyone look so horrible. His face

was actually twisted with rage. He began to curse me—it was dreadful . . ." Her voice shook.

"So what did you do?"

"I ran away. I just ran out of the room—out of the building. I couldn't think straight. I just needed—I don't know what—someone to tell, I suppose, but not anyone in the office, I couldn't face them!"

She buried her face in her hands for a moment and then looked up at me. "Have I been very stupid, Sheila?" she asked.

"No, of course you haven't."

"I should have stayed to make sure he was all right, though, shouldn't I?"

"It sounds to me, from what you've said, that he was *perfectly* all right!"

"Yes, but I should have faced what I'd done."

"You are the victim," I said firmly. "There is absolutely no reason why you should feel guilty."

Thea gave me a wan smile. "Thank you," she said.

I got up from the sofa. "I'm going to make us a cup of tea," I said, "and then I'm going to ring Hugh and say you won't be in for the rest of the day."

She seemed better after she had drunk her tea, so I left her in the sitting room and went into the study to telephone.

"May I speak to Mr. Barber, please?"

I thought the girl's voice was rather odd, polite but with a note of suppressed excitement.

"Mr. Barber isn't in the office at the moment. Who is calling, please? Can I take a message?"

I gave her my name and then asked for Jonah.

"Jonah? It's Sheila. I've got Thea here. I can't go into details just now, but I'm afraid she isn't feeling very well."

"She's with you! We've been ringing, trying to find her, and when she wasn't at home we wondered . . ." Jonah's voice was odd, too. "Look, Sheila, something has happened here and the police need to speak to her right away."

"The police! What on earth do you mean? Don't say that awful man made a complaint—I can't believe it!"

"The police are here because Gordon Masefield's been murdered."

For a moment I couldn't take in what he said.

"But he can't be—he was all right. Jonah, what on earth has happened?"

"Jackie found him. She went into his room to fetch some papers and there he was on the floor with his head bashed in."

"Bashed in?"

"Yes. Someone had hit him over the head with the heavy metal lamp that he had on his desk. It was very messy—poor Jackie's absolutely distraught."

I spared a moment's pity for the poor girl who probably thought she was in love with him. "Look, Jonah, this is all absolutely awful. Thea came to me in great distress." I explained what had happened and then went on. "And now you say Gordon

Masefield's been murdered and the police want to talk to Thea. I simply don't understand."

Jonah's voice was subdued. "Apparently Jackie and Sally saw Thea rushing downstairs looking very upset and then she dashed out of the building without any sort of explanation. So, later on, when Jackie went in and found Gordon dead—well, you can imagine what everyone is thinking."

"The police as well."

"That's right."

"I see. I'd better go and tell Thea what's happened. Perhaps you could tell the police that she's here if they want to talk to her. I'd rather she didn't go back to the office today."

"Yes, all right. I'll do that."

"Thank you, Jonah."

I went slowly back into the sitting room. Thea was standing by the window looking out at the garden.

"It's a beautiful day," she said with a tight little smile. "A perfect summer's day."

I went over and put my arm round her. "Thea, something dreadful has happened. Gordon Masefield's dead."

I felt her stiffen with shock. "No," she said. "No, he can't be. He was alive when I left him. "I *know* he was all right!"

"No, it's not that. He's been murdered. After you left, someone killed him."

She shook her head. "No, it's not possible! How could that happen?"

I led her over to the sofa and made her sit down.

"My dear, I simply don't know. It's all such a muddle."

She looked at me in bewilderment. "You're sure?" she asked. "You're sure they said murder?"

I nodded. "Jonah said that the police want to speak to you. They're coming here to see you."

"To see me? Yes. I suppose they will . . . Sheila"—there was panic in her voice—"they will believe me, won't they? About the accident, I mean."

"Yes, I'm sure they will," I said soothingly, but when I thought of the questions they would ask her and of the answers she would have to give them I felt nothing but hopelessness and despair.

Chapter Five

When the police car drew up in the drive and Inspector Bridges got out, my heart sank. He had taken over while Roger was away and, according to Rosemary who had tried to make a friendly gesture by inviting him to dinner, was both ill-mannered and arrogant.

"He said," Rosemary told me, her voice rising sharply in indignation, "that he didn't believe in making social contacts with the general public as it might lead to some sort of embarrassing situation. As if he expected I might be arrested for shoplifting or something and expect him to bail me out! He's obviously got a very high opinion of himself and I think he wants to use his time here to make his mark—though what he thinks is going to happen in Taviscombe, I can't imagine!"

Well, something quite important had happened and Inspector Bridges would certainly want to show that he was in control.

The doorbell rang and then there was a rapping on the door, as if the mere act of ringing the bell was not a sufficiently peremptory summons.

I looked across at Thea. "It will be all right," I said. "Just tell them what happened."

I opened the door and found that Inspector Bridges had been joined by a constable who stood respectfully one pace behind him.

"Good afternoon, Inspector," I said. "Do come in. Miss Wyatt is in the sitting room. I do apologize for bringing you out here, but she has been greatly upset and is not feeling very well."

He brushed my explanation aside, said brusquely, "In here, is she?" and walked, in front of me, into the room. The constable stood back to let me go in and I smiled at him.

"Good afternoon, Constable Bertram. How is your mother? I was so sorry to hear that she'd been in the hospital."

Inspector Bridges turned back to give me a sharp look, as if he suspected me of trying to subvert the course of justice by this polite enquiry. I followed them into the room. Thea was sitting on the sofa looking very apprehensive. I went over to her and took her hand.

"This is Inspector Bridges, Thea, who would like to ask you a few questions."

She looked appealingly at me. "You will stay, won't you, Sheila?"

"That won't be possible," the inspector said.

"Thea is my son's fiancée," I began, but he interrupted me.

"Police procedure, Mrs. -er . . ."

"Malory," I said. "Sheila Malory."

"Very well, Mrs. Malory," he pronounced my

name carefully as if it was somehow distasteful to him. "If you would kindly leave us." He looked across at Constable Bertram, who opened the door and gave me an apologetic smile as I went past him. I turned in the doorway and said to Thea, "I'll phone Michael and let him know what's happened." Constable Bertram closed the door behind me.

It's a strange feeling to be shut out of a room in your own house and it was with mingled feelings of resentment and apprehension that I telephoned Michael and told him what had happened.

"How is she?" he demanded.

"Upset, as you'd imagine, but she was calming down a bit until that Inspector Bridges arrived. *Not* a very sympathetic person, I'm afraid."

"I'm coming home right away. Tell her not to worry about anything. God! That bastard Masefield—if someone else hadn't killed him, I would!"

"Just come home," I said. "Thea needs you."

I wandered back into the hall. In other circumstances I might have put the kettle on, but I didn't feel that Inspector Bridges was the sort of man who would welcome the offer of a nice cup of tea. Foss came through from the kitchen where he had been inspecting his saucer for any food that might have materialized there since he last visited it. He uttered his usual plaintive food-demanding cry and I picked him up and took him back into the kitchen. I had just opened a tin and tipped the contents into a dish when I heard the door of the sitting room open. I hastily put the dish on the floor and went into the hall. Inspector Bridges, Constable Bertram, and Thea were all at the front door. Thea looked absolutely terrified.

"What's happened?" I asked in bewilderment.

"Miss Wyatt is accompanying us to the station for further questioning," the inspector said.

"But that's ridiculous!" I burst out. "I'm sure she's already told you everything that happened . . ."

He paid absolutely no attention to what I was saying, but opened the door and led Thea away. I ran outside behind them and called to Thea. "I've phoned Michael. He's coming back now—he'll know what to do. Don't worry, everything will be all right."

She gave me a frightened little smile and got into the back of the police car. As if in a dream I watched the car pass down the drive, out into the road, and vanish from sight. I stood there for a while simply not knowing what to do, then I walked slowly into the house and waited for Michael to come home.

He arrived quite soon after, though it seemed like an age.

"Where is she? Is she all right?"

"Michael, come in and sit down. They've taken her down to the police station. For further questioning, he said."

"Oh God! What happened? What did they say to her?"

"I don't know. The inspector wouldn't let me stay in the room."

Michael hadn't sat down but was pacing up and down in an agitated way.

"Do you think they *suspect* her? How did they seem with her?"

"Darling, I don't know. It all happened so quickly and that man Bridges hardly let me get a word in to ask a question or anything, and poor Thea didn't have a chance to tell me either."

"I must get down there now. No, hang on, I'm not thinking properly—she should be properly represented. Did they say anything about a solicitor for her?"

"I really don't know. As I said, they simply took her away. It was awful!"

Michael went toward the phone. "I'll get hold of Edward, he's the best person I know for criminal cases." Edward is the senior partner in Michael's firm.

Michael's last words suddenly brought home to me the full realization of what had happened. "You don't think the inspector really thinks *Thea* murdered Gordon Masefield?" I asked.

"I don't know," Michael said grimly, "but it's beginning to look like it."

He dialed a number and embarked on a conversation, full of legal terms, which I couldn't really follow.

"Right," he said, putting down the phone. "Edward's on his way to the police station. I'll meet him there."

"Shall I come, too?"

"No, you stay here. I'll ring you if there's any news. Good-bye, Ma."

He transferred his mobile phone from his briefcase to his pocket and was gone.

I couldn't settle to anything. I went from room to room, just wandering about. The animals, sensing that something was wrong, were restless too. Foss sat on a windowsill in the hall watching me anxiously, while Tris pawed at my skirt and whined softly. I stooped to pat him.

"It's all right, old boy," I said. "It's going to be all right." But the memory of Thea's frightened white face and Michael's stricken look were still with me.

What seemed like hours later (I'd lost all track of time) Michael came back. He looked dreadful. "They're keeping her there overnight for further questioning," he said.

"There?" I asked. "In *prison*!"

"Yes."

"But they can't!"

"I'm afraid they can."

His voice was bleak and I could tell that he was near to tears. I went over and put my arms round him. "Oh, darling! I'm so sorry. Poor Thea! Is she all right? Were you able to see her?"

"Edward did. He said she seemed dazed—not surprising, really. Oh, Ma, it's so *awful*!"

"I know, darling, I know."

We stood for a while not saying anything, just

trying to comfort each other. Then I said, "I must get some food."

"No, really, Ma, I couldn't . . ."

"You have to have something—just some soup and cheese. And actually I need to *do* something." I heated up a tin of soup and put out some bread and cheese and took it on trays back to the sitting room.

"And a drink," I said. "We both need a drink. Pour us something, darling, please. So what did Edward say?"

"Not a lot." Michael's voice was steadier. "He seems to think that this Bridges man is trying to make a case out against Thea because he hasn't got any other obvious suspects. Edward thinks he's the sort of not-very-bright man who, once he gets hold of an idea, refuses to admit that he might be wrong."

"Oh dear."

We didn't talk much after that. There seemed very little that we could say. We had just finished eating when the doorbell rang.

"Get rid of them, please, Ma," Michael said. "I don't think I could bear to talk to anyone just now."

I got up and went to the door. It was Jonah.

"I hope you don't mind me coming round so late," he said, "but I thought you and Michael would want to know what happened this afternoon."

"Oh, Jonah, how good of you. Please come in. I don't know if you've heard—they've held Thea at the police station for what they call further questioning."

"Yes, Edward telephoned me just now. That's why I thought I'd better come and put you in the picture." He went over to where Michael was sitting. "Mike, I'm really sorry about all this. Obviously there's been some bloody stupid mistake . . ." He sat down and I gave him a glass of beer and he went on. "I'd better begin at the beginning, I suppose. It was all pretty confusing." He drank a little of his beer. "Well now. You know that Thea and I and Gordon all have offices on the second floor. There are these three smallish offices and the closed file storeroom"—he turned to me—"where all the back files and deeds and stuff are kept. That's all at the front, by the front staircase. And then at the back there's Hugh's large office and the small back staircase." He looked at me enquiringly and I nodded.

"Right. Well, just before three, as I told you on the phone, Thea rushed down the front stairs, past reception and out into the street. She was obviously very upset about something. Jackie said she thought she was in tears. Sally got up and went out after her, to see if she was all right, but she'd disappeared down the street. As you can imagine, they were both very concerned, but there was nothing they could do and they were pretty busy, so they went back to what they were doing. Round about four o'clock Hugh telephoned. He was with a client and wanted a check on some figures. Gordon had the file so he told Jackie to go and ask him to look up the relevant paragraphs and phone him back straightaway. Jackie went into Gordon's office and—well, found him there. Like I said, he'd been bashed over the head with this metal lamp. Poor girl, she was in a dreadful state, more or less in hysterics. The other girls rallied round to look after her and I called the police."

He emptied his glass and put it on the table. "I must say I didn't take to this man Bridges at all— very brusque and officious. He was pretty unpleasant to Jackie, kept on and on at her, when it was quite obvious she was in no state to answer questions. He grilled us all—Where were we? What were we doing? What did we see? All perfectly reasonable questions, but his manner . . . Anyway, when he heard about Thea rushing out like that, that was it! He seemed to think that we knew where she was, kept on about it, so when you phoned to say that she was with you, he was onto that in a flash. I'm sorry I couldn't prepare you better for when he turned up, but he was at my elbow while I was taking the call so I couldn't say anything."

"He just marched her off," I said. "It was like a nightmare."

"Well, then Hugh came back and then there were the SOCO people with all their paraphernalia— everyone was talking at once and it was pretty well total confusion. Poor old Hugh just didn't seem able to take it in. He kept saying it must have been an accident, and then when the inspector went on about Thea he was really upset . . ."

"I'm afraid Hugh's had more than his share of trouble this last year," I said. "What with Lois and everything. It's so unfair, he's such a nice man."

Jonah stood up. "That's about all," he said. "I must go and let you both get some rest. You must be exhausted after all this." He turned to Michael. "I'm glad you got Edward for Thea," he said. "Hugh wanted to do it, of course, but he knows that Edward is the expert."

"Yes," Michael said, "he's good. Jonah, thanks for coming. It's helped to know just how things happened."

"I'll keep you posted about how things go in the office and what the police are up to there."

I got up to go to the door with him. "Thank you, Jonah. It was so good of you to come. How's Caroline? When's the baby due?"

"About ten weeks now, so she's a bit uncomfortable, especially in the hot weather."

"Give her our love."

As I closed the door behind him I suddenly became aware of how tired I was. The thought of seeing to the animals and getting myself to bed seemed almost intolerable. I went back wearily into the sitting room.

"I'm going up now, darling," I said. "I think you ought to go to bed as well, you must be exhausted."

"Yes, you're probably right. Though I don't think I'll sleep."

"Do you want something? I've still got some of

those tablets I had when I had that bad go of toothache."

"No, I'll be all right. You go on up—I won't be long."

I fed Foss and Tris and settled them for the night and got thankfully into bed, but like Michael I couldn't sleep. The thought of Thea shut up in a prison cell haunted me. Would it be a cell like the ones in television plays, with a hard bunk and a lavatory in the corner? I had no idea what our local police station had to offer in the way of accommodations for prisoners. But the fact remained that a key had been turned in a lock and Thea *was* a prisoner, in those miserable surroundings, frightened and alone.

I was glad to get up next morning. The sun was shining and the garden outside looked fresh and green, the flowers seemed to be particularly brightly colored and the birds especially full of song. It seemed ironic that the world should seem so beautiful on a day that promised to be at the best stressful and at the worst unbearable.

Michael went off to work early to have a consultation with Edward and I tried to get on with those household tasks that couldn't be put off till another day. I half expected to hear from Michael but the phone didn't ring and by ten o'clock I could bear my own thoughts no longer and called Rosemary to tell her what had happened.

"Oh, Sheila, no! I don't believe it! That wretched man! Shall I come round?"

I accepted gratefully and when we were both seated at the kitchen table, our usual place for serious discussion, with our cups of coffee, I felt much better. There is something about the actual physical presence of one's oldest friend (and Rosemary and I have been friends for nearly fifty years), the sort of friend to whom you can say things that you can't even say to your own family, that brings the best kind of comfort—a blend of familiarity, warmth, and a sort of continuity that no one else can give.

"Oh, if only Roger were here!" Rosemary lamented. "He would never have jumped to the wrong conclusion like this!"

"I do see," I said, feebly attempting to be fair, "that the fact that Thea pushed Gordon Masefield like that and he cut his head might make the inspector suspicious. Especially when he doesn't have any other suspects."

"Well, that's ridiculous," Rosemary said. "Solicitors' offices are always *seething* with ill will. I bet there are half a dozen people there with much stronger motives than poor Thea."

"Well, Gordon Masefield does seem to have been a thoroughly unpleasant man," I agreed. "But," I went on gloomily, "according to Edward, Inspector Bridges is the sort of person who won't admit he's made a mistake, and, now that he's more or less publicly announced that he thinks Thea's guilty, he'd probably think it would make him lose face to say that he was wrong."

"He won't *charge* her, surely? I mean, he'd have

to have some sort of proper evidence to do that, wouldn't he?"

"I'd hope so, but I really don't know."

"At least she's got Edward to advise her."

"I know. It's such a great comfort."

I was really pleased, therefore, when Edward came to see me later that afternoon.

"Michael told me how upset you are about all this, so I thought I'd just come and give you a general idea of what's happening."

"Oh, Edward, that *is* kind of you. I do appreciate it. Please sit down. Will you have a cup of tea?"

"I'd love one, but let me come and talk to you while you make it."

He sat at the kitchen table with the easy familiarity of an old friend, which, of course, is what he is. Edward Drayton was my husband's junior partner and when Peter was ill for so long he was absolutely marvelous, not just in the office, but as a friend, and, since Michael was away at school, he helped me a lot with various difficult things after Peter's death. He's always taken a great interest in Michael and was really pleased when he asked if he could join the firm as an articled clerk when he finished at the College of Law. They've always got on really well. Michael looks on Edward as a sort of father figure, asking and actually taking his advice and Edward appreciates Michael's intelligence and loyalty to the firm. I looked at the large, untidy, bearlike figure sitting at the table. Even the most well-cut suit looks somehow rumpled when Edward has worn it for a few hours, his tie has the habit of sliding to one side, and his thick mane of hair resists all attempts at control, springing energetically from his large leonine head. But such is the warmth of his personality and the kindness of his nature that his clients admire and respect him and his staff adore him.

"Michael is taking this really well," Edward said. "Of course he's worried sick, as who wouldn't be in a situation like this, but he's managing to look at things quite clearly and that is being a great help to Thea. Now, as you know, she has been detained for questioning."

"They can't hold her for more than seventy something hours, isn't it?"

"Yes, but the police can extend the period if they feel it is necessary." He leaned forward. "The thing to hold onto is that they haven't charged her yet, so she's still being held at the local station."

"But they *couldn't* charge her, surely? They haven't any evidence."

"Not as such, but I'm afraid we have to face up to the fact that Thea is in a very precarious position. She has admitted to an assault on Gordon Masefield . . ."

"But surely . . ."

"Technically it was an assault. And yes, it was self-defense. But you do see that the police case must be that she went further than that and, perhaps in a fit of panic, she picked up the lamp and struck him with it, thus causing his death."

"*Could* a woman have hit him hard enough with that lamp to kill him?"

"Yes, apparently it didn't require a great deal of strength. A woman could certainly have done it."

"Oh dear." I thought for a moment and then I asked, "Have they got the pathology report? I mean, can't they differentiate between the two blows—where he banged his head on the desk and where he was actually hit? Surely they can tell if they were done at different times?"

"Not necessarily. If the two incidents happened fairly close to each other, then I doubt if they could tell. But as far as I know, the report isn't in yet."

"Poor Thea, it must be ghastly for her. Isn't there any way we can get her out of there?"

"Well, as I say, they haven't charged her. But, in any case, I don't think there would be any chance of bail since it is a question of murder, or at the least, manslaughter."

"Manslaughter?"

"Manslaughter—self-defense, no intent to kill."

"But she didn't *do* it!" I shook my head in frustration. "How is she, Edward? How is she taking it all?"

"She's better today. Yesterday she was very distressed—first of all the business with Gordon Masefield and then being taken off like that. But today, when I saw her, she was much calmer. She knows that we are all doing everything we can to get her released, and she is trying to be patient and brave about it. Being a solicitor herself and knowing the law is a mixed blessing—she can see both the good and the bad side of the situation." He smiled. "She is a remarkable girl. Michael is very lucky."

"If only there was something we could *do*!"

"Well, you could find the real murderer. *Someone* killed Gordon Masefield and we have the advantage over Inspector Bridges of knowing that it wasn't Thea."

Chapter Six

"Edward's right," Michael said when I told him. "We know that Thea didn't kill Masefield, so someone else must have."

"He was such an unpleasant man—he must have had a lot of enemies in the office," I said hopefully. "And solicitors quite often upset their clients as well. There was that case the other day when someone *shot* his solicitor because he didn't get the result he wanted."

"Yes, Ma." Michael smiled. "But I think you'll find that was an exception. Still, I agree about the enemies. We must try and follow that up."

"It'll be awkward, though," I said, "trying to find things out about Barber and Freeman."

"Oh, I don't know. Jonah will do everything he can to help and you know Hugh Barber quite well, I'm sure he'll help all he can. He's very fond of Thea."

"Yes, that's true. Actually, the first thing we need to know is where everyone was when it happened. Thea was on her way here, of course, and I think Hugh was out because he wasn't there when I tried to ring him about Thea and I got through to Jonah instead . . ."

Michael got up. "I'll give Jonah a ring and ask him to make a list of where everyone was, then we can start to eliminate people."

"Always supposing it *was* someone in the office. It could have been someone from outside."

"Yes, well, we'll cross that bridge when we come to it. First things first."

"Right, then you go and ring Jonah and I'll see to supper. Oh dear, I wonder what the *food* is like at that police station?"

"I expect the food is the least of Thea's worries," Michael said.

"Oh, I know, darling—I didn't mean . . ."

"It's all right, Ma, I know what you meant. Call me when it's ready."

When we explained, Jonah was eager to help. He made out a list of all the people at Barber and Freeman and took it round to Michael's office the next day. It's just as well we had something to occupy our minds because that morning Edward told Michael that Inspector Bridges had formally charged Thea with the murder of Gordon Masefield.

He came home at lunchtime to tell me and I was shocked to see how ill he looked.

"They've taken her to Shepton Mallet," he said. "That's where they keep the remand prisoners."

"Oh, darling." I couldn't think of anything to say.

"Oh, Ma, it's so bloody *awful*." I saw the tears in

his eyes as he buried his face in his hands and I remembered a teenage boy crying for the death of his father. I put my arms around him as I had done then and we cried together.

After a while, when we were both more composed, Michael said, "Well at least I'll be able to visit her now, see how she is."

"Yes, that will be something. Tell her we're really going to find out who the murderer is."

That evening we looked at Jonah's list.

As I had remembered, Hugh had been out seeing a client, and his partner Jason Chapman had been out as well. So Hugh's office, upstairs, next to Gordon Masefield's, had been empty. The other two offices on that floor belonged to Jonah and Thea. Jonah said he'd been working in his office all afternoon and hadn't heard anything at all until Jackie found Gordon and started screaming. Then he'd rushed out to see what the fuss was about and had been the first person—after Jackie—to see the body.

Of the offices downstairs, Jason Chapman's was empty, of course, and the legal executive, Eileen Newton, was in the office next to his. She said that she'd been in there all afternoon, and she too came out when the commotion started. The two secretaries, Jackie and Carol, were in the large office at the back and Sally, the receptionist, was in the open waiting area at the front. "Now let me get this straight," I said. "There are two entrances—one at the front, leading from the street into reception, and one at the back in the secretaries' room that leads out into that lane at the back of the building, so anyone coming or going would have been seen by either Sally at the front or Jackie and Carol at the back?"

"Yes, that's right."

"And there are two staircases, the one at the front going up from the reception area and the back staircase going up from the corridor outside the secretaries' room?"

"That's it."

"It's pretty odd, isn't it, that Jonah didn't hear anything? I mean, things falling over and Gordon crashing to the floor—twice, as it happens."

"Well, Gordon's room, as I remember it, is across quite a big landing from Jonah's and between them there's the room where the old files are kept. Anyway, Jonah said that on that afternoon he had his door shut."

"What do you mean, 'on that afternoon?'"

"In solicitors' offices we usually leave our doors open unless we have a client with us, or there is some special reason for having it shut."

"And what was Jonah doing, do we know?"

"Oh, he had a particularly tricky tax case to prepare and he needed to concentrate. I can quite understand why he didn't hear anything. When you're desperately trying to juggle with calculators and computer printouts, you probably wouldn't notice the end of the world! Why? You surely don't think that *Jonah* had anything to do with all this?"

"No, of course not. I just wondered, that's all." I sighed. "Oh dear, I do wish we could talk to everyone and see exactly where they were when it happened. Inspector Bridges does have an unfair advantage."

"I think Jonah might be able to do that for us. From what I can gather, everyone there liked Thea very much and they don't believe she's guilty, so I'm sure they'll cooperate."

"Except the murderer," I pointed out, "who'd be lying anyway."

"Certainly no one has a good word to say for Gordon Masefield—oh, except Jackie, of course."

"Well, the poor girl thought she was in love with him. Though why I'm saying poor girl I don't know, because she knew perfectly well that he was married and had a small child. Which reminds me, what about his wife?"

"Wendy? I don't know."

"She must be very upset. Fortunately, I think she's got quite a large family so it's to be hoped that they'll help her."

"That's right, she's got three brothers. I know Steve, he's the youngest, he sometimes comes to the clay-shoot."

"Of course, she was Wendy Lewis! I remember now. Kathleen Lewis, that's her mother, used to be very friendly with Anthea. I'll give her a ring tomorrow and see what I can pick up there."

"Do you think Wendy knew Gordon was playing around?"

"Oh, I'm sure she did. *We* all knew what he was like—it was common knowledge, after all. Jackie wasn't the first, was she? I'm quite sure *someone* made it their business to tell Wendy."

"There might be a motive there," Michael said hopefully.

"Oh, I'm sure we can find umpteen motives! It's just that the horrible Bridges man decided not to look further than the end of his nose! Don't you worry, love, we'll get to the bottom of this!"

"Thanks, Ma," Michael said gratefully. "You're right, of course, we must just keep on looking."

I ran into Hugh the next day when I was waiting to cross the Avenue. They're digging up all that stretch of road—something to do with a collapsed culvert and it's been going on for weeks now—and there's always a great buildup of traffic there.

"Sheila!" Hugh came up behind me. "I was going to call and see you today."

"Hugh, how are you?"

I was really shocked at his appearance. Even in the short time since I last saw him he seemed to have aged. He looked gaunt and thin and his face was parchment-gray.

"Oh well, you know how things have been. Look, we can't talk here, and I do want to have a word with you." He looked at his watch. "It's just after twelve, how about a drink? Unless you'd rather go to the Buttery for a coffee?"

"A drink would be nice."

"Right, let's go to the King's Head, it's usually quiet in there."

When he had got our drinks he said, "First of all,

Sheila, I want you to know how sorry I am about Thea. I had a word with Michael on the phone and, as I say, I was coming to see you. I can imagine what you've both been going through."

"It has been awful," I said. "Michael's been wonderful about it, but, of course, he's been dreadfully upset."

"No one believes for a moment that she did it," Hugh said earnestly. "It's obviously all a terrible mistake. Inspector Bridges simply jumped to the wrong conclusion."

"Yes. I can't believe that Roger Eliot would have arrested her like that, with no real evidence."

"How is she? Who has seen her?"

"Well, Edward, obviously, and Michael is trying to get to see her today. They've taken her to Shepton Mallet, you know."

"Yes, I had heard. How is she? Did Edward say?"

"He said that she was bearing up very well, all things considered, but it's bound to be a terrible experience for her just being in that place, let alone wondering what's going to happen to her at the trial."

He nodded sympathetically. "I just wish there was *something* I could do to help. Of course I told the inspector what sort of person she is and how it's impossible that she could have killed anyone, but you know what he's like . . ."

I nodded.

"Everyone in the office is very shocked, naturally." He paused for a moment and then said, "To be honest with you, Sheila, Gordon Masefield wasn't much liked, and I'm afraid some of his work was— well, how shall I put it?—unreliable, shall I say. Jason and I had more or less come to the conclusion that we would have to dispense with his services. There were other things, too. I can't go into details, obviously, but I fear that his behavior toward Thea was not the only instance of the way he conducted himself, you know what I mean?"

"I see."

"I told the inspector all this—I thought it might alter his mind about Thea—but, alas, he didn't seem to attach any importance to it."

"No," I said despondently, "I don't suppose he did."

"He has interviewed everyone in the office and examined the scene of the crime, as it were, but that seems to be that. I'm so sorry, Sheila."

"Well, thank you for doing what you have, Hugh, and for your sympathy."

We sipped our drinks in silence and then I asked, "How is Lois?"

He shook his head. "It's not good news, I'm afraid. The specialist seems to think it won't be long now."

"Oh, Hugh, I *am* sorry. How is she in herself?"

"Not too bad. She doesn't need the nurse at present—you know we had to have one living in for a while." His expression brightened. "In fact the specialist says that she can go on this cruise she's set her heart on."

"Cruise?"

"Yes. It's something rather special. We fly out to Barbados on the Concorde, and then cruise around the Caribbean, calling at the various islands and on to bits of South America."

"It sounds very glamorous. Concorde, too!"

"Well, it had to be really because Lois couldn't stand a seven-hour flight. And, well, that's what she wanted."

"Yes, of course."

"She loves the sun. She always feels better in a hot climate." He smiled. "Unlike Taviscombe!"

"This summer has been rather dire," I agreed.

"That's why I specially wanted her to have this trip."

"I'm so glad she's well enough to go. And," I said, "I hope it will do you good as well. If you'll forgive my saying so, you look as if *you* could do with a good rest."

"I must admit, it has been something of a strain these last few months, and then this dreadful thing happening at the office."

There was a muffled ringing noise and Hugh reached into his breast pocket and brought out a mobile phone.

"Hello? Lois? You need what? No, of course I hadn't forgotten. I'm going to get it now and you shall have it this evening. No, I won't be late—six o'clock at the latest. Well, ask Marguerite to come in for tea or for a drink or something. Yes—well, all right, I'll leave early. I expect I can rearrange my appointments. What about lunch? Has Mrs. Loden left you something nice? Oh, I'm sure it's splendid, crab salad sounds delicious . . . All right, darling, I'll see you soon. Try and have a little rest this afternoon . . . Yes, all right . . . good-bye."

Hugh put the phone away and gave me an apologetic smile. "I'm so sorry," he said. "I always have to keep my mobile switched on in case Lois wants something urgently."

"It's marvelous to be able to keep in touch like that," I said.

"Yes. I do find it reassuring and Lois . . . well, she gets very bored all by herself all day, not being able to do what she used to do."

From what I remember of Lois Barber in the days before her illness, she didn't do a great deal except go on expensive shopping trips to London, and Paris, even, and play a lot of bridge. "Does she still play bridge?" I asked Hugh.

He sighed. "No, not any more. Since she came out of hospital last she seems to have lost interest, and then some of her friends at the bridge club have moved away and she doesn't care for the new people."

"What a shame. Still, I don't suppose she has much energy for things like that. Do, please, remember me to her and say that I hope she enjoys the trip." I gathered up my bag and shopping bag. "I must be going. Thank you so much for the drink."

Hugh stood up. "Once again, Sheila, I am so very sorry about Thea. If there's anything I can do."

"Thank you, Hugh. You're very kind."

"I do feel badly about going away just now . . ."

"No, you have to do what you can for Lois, we do understand that. Try and relax a little—though I know that won't be easy. If I don't see you before you go, bon voyage!" I held out my hand and Hugh took it in both of his.

"Thank you, Sheila, that is very understanding of you. Please give my best to Michael and tell Thea when you see her that I *know* everything will come right in the end."

"Oh dear, poor Hugh," Rosemary said when she called on me that afternoon. "He must feel awful going away just now, but if Lois has made up her mind that's what she wants, then that's what he'll have to do."

"Well, if the end is as near as he says . . ."

"Yes, I suppose so. The trouble is, I've never liked Lois and I can't suddenly start liking her just because she's going to die."

"I do know what you mean—it's Hugh one feels really sorry for. He's so devoted to her. I can't imagine how he's going to cope when she goes."

"It's a pity they never had any children, though I would pity any child of Lois's! But Hugh will have no one. He hasn't any relations at all, has he?"

"I think there's a cousin in New Zealand, but no one over here."

"Poor soul. And then all this horrible business at the office . . ." Rosemary broke off and looked at me with some concern. "I'm sorry, Sheila. I shouldn't have reminded you."

"No, really, we're sort of coming to terms with it.

Well, Michael's very uptight, naturally, though he's been a bit better since he was able to see Thea."

"How is she? What is it like in that place?"

"Prison? Well, it could be worse, I gather. She's sort of keeping her head down and getting by. *She's* comforting Michael, by all accounts, bless her!" I leaned forward and moved Tris slightly so that he wasn't sitting on my feet. "Rosemary," I asked, "when's Roger due back?"

"About a week now, I think. I haven't heard from them for a while because they were traveling about, but they should be in Florida on Monday." She looked at me enquiringly. "Do you want me to phone him about Thea?"

I shook my head. "I don't know. I don't think so. No, it wouldn't be right. He'll be home soon enough. Do you think he'll be able to take the case over when he does come back?"

"I honestly don't know how these things work, but he *is* this man Bridges's superior officer and if he thinks a mistake has been made, then he'll certainly say so!"

"Well, that's a comfort, anyway." I got to my feet. "I'll go and put the kettle on. Oh dear, I wish I knew how all this was going to end."

"It will be all right," Rosemary said firmly.

"That's what Hugh said." I sighed as I went out of the room. "I just wish I could believe it, too."

Chapter Seven

I hate taking Foss to the vet, even if it's only for something minor like an injection. He bellows at the top of his voice all the way there in the car, (presumably demanding that Amnesty International should release him from the cage I've had to put him in), he wails pathetically (a higher note this and very effective at eliciting sympathy) while we are in the waiting room, he growls and hisses at poor Simon the vet, and when we get home Tris won't have anything to do with him for ages because he smells of disinfectant and vets. One really does need to feel quite strong even to contemplate it. Actually it was only a booster injection but we still went through the whole performance.

When we got there the waiting room was quite full ("Simon's had to go out to see to a horse," the receptionist said resignedly) and I put Foss's cage up on one of the chairs well away from a couple of dogs who showed an interest in it. The owner of one of the dogs, a depressed-looking Labrador, came over and sat beside me and I saw that it was Miriam Yates.

"Hello, Sheila," she said, "I thought it was you."

There never is any answer to that sort of remark so I simply smiled and waited for her usual flood of conversation. Miriam is one of Taviscombe's greatest gossips, so I waited with some trepidation for what she might say about the Gordon Masefield affair. Sure enough, after a brisk review of the marital status of most of her acquaintance and a diatribe about the iniquities of the local authorities in respect to the banding of her council tax, she finally got around to it.

"And then that dreadful murder! In a solicitor's office, too—it somehow seems to make it worse, don't you think? Poor Hugh Barber, as if he hadn't got enough to worry about with that wife of his! Mind you, I'm not surprised. Well, you see, we knew Gordon Masefield." She moved her chair nearer mine and lowered her voice presumably for dramatic effect since the other occupants of the waiting room all seemed to be engrossed in copies of *Country Life* and *Hello Magazine*.

"He went out for a while with my daughter Karen. You remember her, don't you? She used to be a hair stylist at Veronique's but she's doing aromatherapy now and she's really enjoying it. I think it's more her *thing*, if you know what I mean. Anyway, he and Karen went out together for a couple of months, but I said to her, 'It's no use, Karen, he's not the sort of man you could ever be *sure* of. Not reliable at all.' Do you know, he'd ring up in the evening, just when she was getting ready to go out with him, and say he couldn't make it. Said he had to see a client, but I found out that he was seeing that Ruth Williams—some client! Oh, I soon found out what sort of person he was and I made Karen finish with him."

She looked at me with an air of triumph, which I acknowledged with a murmur of approval. "I think Karen was a bit upset when he married Wendy Lewis—an insipid sort of girl, we couldn't think what he saw in her, but then, of course, with the baby arriving so early . . . well!" Foss, who had been unusually silent, gave a sudden wail and Miriam looked at him briefly before she went on. "But marriage wasn't going to change *him* now, was it? I've heard all sorts of stories, and I expect you have too. But do you know who I saw him with in Taunton a couple of weeks ago? You'll not believe it!" I leaned forward, in my turn anxious not to miss anything. "Well." Miriam settled herself more comfortably in her chair as she warmed to her story. "Well, Phyllis Barker and I had been shopping—nothing in the sales this time, a great disappointment, just bought-in stuff, no real bargains—anyway, we were quite worn out with traipsing about Taunton all morning, so we thought we'd give ourselves a little treat and try that wine bar, you know, the one at the bottom of East Reach. It's quite fashionable. Karen says you can't get into it on Saturday nights, but this was a Tuesday lunchtime so it was really quite empty. *But* who should I see tucked away in a corner but Master Masefield, and who should be with him but Laura Chapman, yes, Jason Chapman's wife!"

I reflected that if Gordon Masefield thought he could get away with conducting his assignations in secret further afield he greatly underestimated the ubiquity of Taviscombe matrons.

"Good gracious!" I said. "But are you sure? I mean, it might have been a perfectly innocent chance meeting."

Miriam laughed scornfully. "There was nothing chance about *that* meeting," she said. "All over each other, they were!"

"Did he see you?" I asked.

"Oh yes, I made sure of that. I went right up to them and said, 'Fancy seeing you here.' He looked thoroughly embarrassed and so did she."

"I can imagine."

"So you see I wasn't really surprised that he came to a bad end. They say it was one of the girls in his office—poor soul, he'd obviously been playing her along like all the rest and it was too much for her."

I offered up a silent prayer of thanks that Michael and Thea hadn't put an announcement of their engagement in any of the papers. Miriam Yates's prying sympathy would have been more than I could have borne. Fortunately Simon put his head round the door and summoned her into his office and I was left to ponder the information she had given me.

"So you see Jason Chapman would have had a perfectly good motive," I said to Michael. "If he knew about his wife and Masefield. I mean, apart from the obvious reason, he'd certainly be even more furious that someone, someone junior in his office, was having an affair with Laura."

"But he was out of the office when it happened."

"Well, do we really know that?" I asked. "From what Edward says, the forensic people haven't been able to give an *exact* time of death, certainly not to within an hour. A lot could have happened in an hour. When did he go out exactly? Can you get Jonah to find out?"

"Good old Jonah," Michael said the next evening. "He's got some times for us."

"Oh, splendid."

"We know that Thea rushed out of the office at about two forty-five. Jackie was in reception talking to Sally and they both saw her and wondered what was up. They're pretty sure of the time because Jackie had come out to reception to collect someone who was coming to see Eileen Newton at two forty-five. What time did Thea arrive here?"

"Oh, about three o'clock—yes, that's right, I heard the grandfather clock in the hall striking when I brought her indoors."

"Right, then. Now Sally says that Chapman went out at three fifteen, so there was a whole half hour between Thea leaving and Chapman going out. He could easily have killed Masefield in that time."

"That's right!" I exclaimed.

"Jackie didn't find the body until just before four o'clock, so he could perfectly well have claimed that he was out when the murder was committed."

"That's terrific!" I said.

Michael grimaced. "No proof, though I *do* wish that there was some way we could find out exactly when the wretched man did die."

"Yes."

"Actually, guess who was in the office that day?"

"Who?"

"Gordon Masefield's wife, Wendy."

"No!"

"No use, I'm afraid. She was in in the morning—she brought some papers he'd left at home."

"Oh, how sickening. Why couldn't it have been the afternoon! Still, there's always Jason Chapman, surely there's something there. If only we could get those times sorted out."

"Yes." Michael was looking thoughtful. "I've got a kind of idea at the back of my mind, but I want to think about it a bit more."

"Right. Well, I'll just get these supper things cleared away. You see if there's anything on the telly." As I began to gather up the plates and put them on the tray I said tentatively, "Are you going to see Thea tomorrow?"

"Yes."

"I don't suppose I could come with you?"

Michael hesitated and then looked a bit embarrassed.

"Well, actually, Ma, I'd rather you didn't."

"Oh."

"It's Thea. When I said that you'd probably like to come with me one visiting day, she said she didn't want you to."

"I see."

"No, look, don't be hurt and upset. It's just that she doesn't want anyone to see her in that place. I don't think she really wants me to go, but she puts up with it for my sake, because she knows that I need to see her, just to keep going."

"Yes, of course. Poor Thea, I *do* understand."

Michael was very quiet and preoccupied for the rest of the evening and, quite early, I went to bed leaving him downstairs with a book open on his lap, which he was obviously not reading.

The following afternoon I was making pastry, up to my wrists in flour, when Michael suddenly appeared.

"Darling! What are you doing home so early?"

I could tell immediately that something had happened; his whole demeanor was different, he was alert and cheerful, quite his old self, and bursting to tell me something.

"Ma, something marvelous has happened! Oh, leave that! Come and sit down, I've got something to tell you!"

I wiped my floury hands on my apron and sat down at the kitchen table.

"What is it, what's happened?"

"Hang on, I must tell you from the beginning. You know I told you that I'd had a thought? Well, I got Jonah to let me have a look round Gordon's office. The police had finished with it, so it was all right. Apparently, what with one thing and another, no one at Barber and Freeman had thought

to see what Gordon had been working on just before he died."

"What about the police?" I asked. "Didn't they
want to know?"

"Bridges was quite sure that he'd got the murderer," Michael said grimly. "He wasn't going to
bother. Anyway I had a word with Jonah and he
had a word with Jason Chapman—Hugh wasn't
there today, I think he's off on that cruise tomorrow—and *he* said it would be okay. So Jonah and I
had a good look through the things on Masefield's
desk, and guess what we found?"

I shook my head.

"No, you won't guess, so I'll tell you. Apparently
after Thea left he'd been working on his computer.
He'd made a call to Lexis—that's the law report
database—and the printout shows that the call was
logged at three thirty!"

"So you mean . . ."

"Thea left the office at two forty-five, Sally and
Jackie saw her!"

"And she was *here* at three o'clock."

"So she's got an alibi, a completely cast-iron
alibi!" Michael cried triumphantly.

"Oh, darling, how *wonderful!*"

"And," he went on, "it's even better. There was a
note on his pad to remind him to send an E-mail to
one of his clients. Jonah phoned the company and
they did get the E-mail and, thank God, they filed
it. That gave the time it was sent as three twenty."
There was a great big smile on his face as I knew
there must be on mine. "Isn't that *brilliant*?"

"Absolutely brilliant," I said.

For a moment we both just stood there too happy to say anything, then I asked, "What happens now?"

"I got onto Edward straightaway and he's going to take the relevant documents—that's the Lexis printout and a photocopy of the E-mail—to Bridges."

"They'll have to let her go, won't they?" I enquired anxiously.

"Yes," Michael said. "There's no way they can keep her now."

"Will you go and fetch her?"

"I hope I can go with Edward. I don't know yet how things will happen."

"What's the time?" I asked. "There will be time to get her out today? It would be awful if she had to spend another night in that place."

"I've got to wait until I hear from Edward. He said he'd ring as soon as he had any news." Michael paused for a moment and then said, "Of course, this gives Jason Chapman an alibi too."

"Who cares!" I said, going back to my pastry. "As long as Thea's free, who cares *who* killed Gordon Masefield!"

Chapter Eight

I'd gone to bed by the time Michael got back that evening, but I was reading (or rather trying to read) and my light was on. There was a tap on the door and Michael's head came round.

"It's okay. She's back."

"Come and tell me all about it," I said.

He came in and sat on the bed. "Edward had arranged everything. We just rolled up and collected her."

"How was she?" I asked.

Michael shrugged. "It's hard to tell. She was very quiet on the drive home. It was pretty much of a surprise for *her,* actually. They hadn't told her she was being released until about an hour before we arrived, so she'd barely had time to get used to the idea, poor love. Edward told her what we'd discovered, about the times and everything, and she seemed just about able to take it in, but she was still pretty dazed."

"Poor child," I exclaimed, "she must be feeling completely disoriented!"

"Edward drove her home and I went in with her,

to see that everything was all right. She didn't want me to stay. She said she just wanted to have a bath and then go to bed and have a proper night's sleep. So I came away."

"I'm sure that was the right thing to do," I said. "You'll have to let her take her time over things, she's going to need a *lot* of time to get over this."

"Yes, I suppose you're right." He gave a tremendous yawn. "God, I'm tired! This day seems to have been forty-eight hours long!"

"Go to bed now or you'll be fit for nothing tomorrow. Good night, darling. I'm so glad Thea is home safely."

I suppose it was inevitable that Thea would take some time to recover from her ordeal. I know Michael found it hard to understand and was impatient to resume their former life. I telephoned her the day after she returned but left it for a few days before I actually called to see her. She was, on the surface, her usual cheerful and friendly self, but I was very conscious that underneath she was still tense and on edge.

"Jason has very kindly said I can have a week off," she said, pouring the coffee. "Longer if I want it."

"That's good."

She passed a cup to me with a hand that trembled slightly. "Actually, Sheila, I'm rather dreading it."

"Going back to the office? I can understand that."

"It's not just the actual *office*—though that will be rather horrible—but I don't know if I can face the people."

I looked at her enquiringly. "In what way?"

"I can't explain, it's a bit complicated. I know I'll feel embarrassed. I mean, everyone will know what happened, why I rushed out like that . . ."

"I don't think you should feel embarrassed about *that*," I said firmly. "That was entirely his fault and you have absolutely nothing to reproach yourself about. And I'm quite sure that everyone will feel that you've had a terrible time and will want to do whatever they can to make up to you for it."

"Yes, well, that might be even worse in a way," Thea said.

"What do you mean?"

"Oh, I don't know. It's just that I'm finding *people* rather difficult to cope with just now." She smiled. "Not you, or Michael—though I'm afraid he's a little uncertain how I'll take things, poor love—but just people in general and certainly more than one at a time."

"I suppose after—that place . . ."

"Prison? Yes. That was one of the worst things about it, never being alone. I hated that."

"How were the other people there?"

"Not bad, really. There were a couple of unpleasant ones, but I just kept my head down and tried not to get in their way . . ." She broke off and I saw that she shuddered a little, as if at some upsetting memory. "It could have been worse, I suppose. Except for the terrible feeling that no one would sort things out and I'd be shut up there, or somewhere like it, for years and years."

"You poor child, I can't imagine how you could bear it!"

"Well, you sort of took one day at a time. But you do see . . ."

"That it will take some time for you to adjust? Yes, I can."

"I *do* want company," Thea said earnestly, "but then when people come, I can't cope. And, again, I can't help going over it again and again in my mind. I can't seem to think of anything else. Nothing else seems real."

"It's a bit like having been in hospital for a long time," I said. "Much worse, of course, but the same principle. You've been part of an entirely enclosed world and, for a while at least, nothing outside that world has any reality for you."

"Yes," she said, "that's it. Sheila, how long will it take to get back to the real world?"

"That will depend on you, but I have an idea that might help."

"What's that?"

"Wait and see. I'll come back tomorrow and we'll see if it works."

When I went back to see Thea the next day I had a large cardboard box with me.

"What on earth?" Thea broke off as muffled sounds came from the box. I opened it and a small head appeared cautiously. Thea reached inside and brought out a small, long-haired silver tabby kitten. "Oh, Sheila!"

"Sale or return," I said, smiling. "I went to see my friend Ella this morning and she had these two rescued kittens. She named this one Smoke and its brother, who's got white feet, is Boots, but I daresay you could call her something else if you'd rather. That's if you want to keep her, that is."

Thea stroked the kitten's fur delicately with one finger and her eyes filled with tears. Holding the little animal close to her she began to cry in earnest. After a while she became calmer and passed the kitten to me, saying, "Poor thing, I've frightened it."

I stroked the little creature and said, "That's better, isn't it?"

She nodded. "Much better," she said. She took out a handkerchief and dried her eyes. "Thank you, Sheila," she said. "Thank you for that and for Smoke." She smiled. "You really are very clever!"

"I expect they call it therapy nowadays," I said. "But one thing I do know—if you've got to look after a kitten, you won't have time to think of anything else!"

"And animals are the perfect company," Thea said, "when humans are too much."

I passed the kitten back to her. "She comes with her own food, earth tray, and cat litter," I said, going over to the cardboard box and taking things out. "But I didn't bring a basket, in case you didn't want to keep her."

Thea laughed, a real laugh I was glad to hear.

"You knew very well," she said, "that the moment I saw her I'd be lost! Anyway, she'll sleep on my bed."

She found a piece of string and twitched it for the kitten, who pounced on it happily.

They were both so absorbed in their game that when I left a little while later they hardly noticed.

"Well, really, Ma!" Michael exclaimed when he got in that evening. "I did hope that when I married Thea I'd be entering an animal-free zone!"

"How did you know?" I asked.

"Thea phoned me at work. She sounded really excited, almost her old self again."

"There you are, then."

"Yes, well, I grant that you are wise and clever and that it's done the trick for Thea, but who's going to have to *live* with the result of your little experiment in psychology?"

"Nonsense," I said briskly. "She's a dear little creature and you'll love her."

"And of course he does," I told Rosemary. "He insisted on going with Thea when she took Smoke to the vet to have her injections. He said that the carrying cage was too heavy for Thea to manage but it was really because he didn't want to be left out!"

"How sweet! I'm so pleased that it seems to have done the trick for Thea. Poor girl, it must have been a terrible ordeal for her."

"Yes. She's not over it yet. She won't talk about it, even to Michael, but she's beginning to relax a little now—that awful *deadness* she had when she first came back seems to have gone, thank goodness, but there's obviously a long way to go. I think she's really dreading going back to work."

"I can imagine."

"Just being in the place where it happened will be bad enough, but I think she's worried about the other people there."

"Surely there's no doubt in anyone's mind . . ."

"No, it's not that. I suppose it's a sort of embarrassment. It's a pity Hugh won't be there—he and Lois have gone on that cruise. He would have made her feel more comfortable."

"Well, I don't suppose anyone will mind if she takes her time about going back."

"No, probably not. Of course," I said thoughtfully, "it would make all the difference if we knew who *did* murder Gordon Masefield. What's happening about the investigation, I wonder?"

"I don't know. I suppose that wretched Inspector Bridges is casting around for somebody else to accuse!"

"Well," I said austerely, "I hope he has some proper evidence the next time he arrests someone."

The days passed and still Thea didn't go back to work. She appeared to be much more her old self and she and Michael seemed happy enough together, but I felt there was a certain constraint about them both and I felt I had to tackle Michael about it.

"*Is* everything all right between you and Thea?" I asked one morning at breakfast.

"What do you mean, all right?"

"Well, I don't know exactly," I said, plugging in the percolator. "It's just that I have a sort of feeling that things aren't. Not quite, anyway."

"We're fine." Michael's voice was muffled as he bent down to get the cereal out of the cupboard and I couldn't see his face.

"Well, if you're sure . . ."

He sprinkled sugar lavishly over the bran flakes, then laid down the spoon and looked at me. "No, you're quite right, of course. Things are a bit—well—different, I suppose. I *know* it'll take time for her to get over things, I do understand that. But although she's miles better—thanks to that damned kitten—I don't think she'll ever really be herself again until whoever it is who murdered that creep Masefield is caught."

I nodded. "I thought it might be that. Has she said so?"

"No. We never refer to it. Perhaps we should. Honestly, I don't know." He suddenly clenched his fists and brought them down on the table. "I don't know what to *do*, Ma. She won't talk about the wedding even. She won't set a date or anything. I'm beginning to wonder if she thinks she's made a mistake and doesn't want to marry me after all."

I shook my head. "No, darling, I'm sure that's not it. I know that if I say you must be patient just one more time you'll go mad, but I'm afraid that's the way it is." I put the toast in the rack and got out the butter. "The fact is that neither of us can possibly imagine what Thea has gone through. Not only the prison—though that must have been really unbearable—but being accused of *murder*. I mean, just think about it! And, as Thea herself said, sitting there day after day and wondering if anyone would ever believe her or if she'd be shut up in that vile place for years and years."

"Yes, I'm sure you're right. It's just that it's so *hard*. I want to help so much and there's so little I can do."

"You're doing your best, and I'm sure Thea is grateful. Anyway," I said, "*you* got Thea out of prison. If you hadn't checked that computer she'd still be there. Come along now and have your breakfast else you'll be late for work."

But as I was making the beds that morning, hampered as usual by Foss burrowing under the bedclothes and having to be turfed out, I was still thinking of Thea and wondering how long it would be before she became her old self again. It seemed to me that she was haunted by the ghost of Gordon Masefield and until that ghost was laid to rest she would never be free. One way to set her free, of course, would be to find out who the real murderer was. It seemed now that the fact of Thea being out of prison wasn't going to be the end of the affair, as I had imagined.

Perhaps we—Michael and I, that is, with Jonah's help perhaps—should really try to solve the murder, since it seemed likely that Inspector Bridges had no other suspects in mind and would probably, in view of his first mistake, be unwilling to make another hasty move.

I was just about to sit down with a pencil and paper to make a list of possible suspects when the phone rang. It was Rosemary.

"Hello, Sheila. Can you come round for coffee? Jilly and Roger and the children are back from America and I'm longing to show you the heavenly things they brought back for Jack and me! They had a marvelous time—Mark and Delia adored Disney World. Actually, I think Jilly loved it too, though she's pretending to be superior about it!"

"Yes, I'd love to. It's just what I need—I was feeling a bit down. I'll be with you in about twenty minutes."

I was suddenly conscious of a tremendous feeling of relief. Perhaps now that Roger was back we stood a proper chance of finding out what had really happened and who actually *had* murdered Gordon Masefield.

Chapter Nine

A few days later Roger came to see me.

"Roger! How lovely! Do come in. Would you like some coffee?"

"I'd love a cup of tea. I longed for a really good cup in America, nice and strong, just like yours."

"Fine. Come into the kitchen while I make it and tell me all about things. Did you have a successful trip?"

"Yes. It was interesting and I got on well with the people over there. I think we can learn something from what they're doing. And of course it was marvelous to have Jilly and the children out there. We had a fabulous time in Florida. We stayed with the sister of the lieutenant I was working with in New York. She and her husband insisted on driving us to Disney World with their children and not just Disney World, she took us all over! They're so amazingly hospitable, aren't they?"

"They're marvelous. When any Americans I know come over here I always feel so *inadequate* after all they've done for me when I've been there!" I poured some water onto the tea and put the cups ready on a tray. "Shall we have it here, or shall I take it through?"

"Oh, here, please." Roger sat down at the kitchen table while I put some biscuits on a plate. "Oh good, chocolate digestives! I've missed those as well."

I poured the tea and sat down opposite him.

"Well," he said, "you can probably guess why I'm here—apart from the tea and biscuits, of course."

"Yes, I think I can."

"I've been to see Miss Wyatt, of course."

"Poor Thea. It really has affected her badly. What will happen now?"

"I asked her if she wanted to take things further but she said she'd rather not."

"Oh dear. Well, yes, I suppose . . . I can see that she just wants to put the whole thing behind her and try and forget it ever happened."

"That was the impression I got, certainly."

We drank our tea in silence for a while, then I said, "But, you see, she doesn't seem *able* to put it behind her."

"What do you mean?"

"I get the feeling that until Gordon Masefield's murderer is actually caught she won't be able to go back to leading a normal life."

"I see."

"Do you really?"

"Yes, I think I do. It's only logical, if you think of it. Although she has an alibi for the time of his death and is thus completely exonerated, because she was actually arrested she feels that she will always be a suspect until the real killer has been discovered."

"But *you* don't think of her as a suspect and I can't believe that anyone at Barber and Freeman does."

"I think that's the way she feels."

"Well then," I said, "you'll have to find the murderer as soon as possible. I don't want to be done out of a spring wedding for Michael and Thea, and that won't be possible if the bride-to-be is still glooming about some tiresome murder!"

Roger laughed. "I'll do my best," he said. "That's really what I wanted to see you about."

I looked at him enquiringly and he laughed.

"Oh, come on, Sheila. You've helped me before and this time you have a special interest."

"That's true."

"You and Michael and Jonah, too, can be very helpful. You were all here when it happened—not halfway round the world like I was—and you were all involved, you and Michael through Thea and Jonah because he works there. And, of course, Michael and Jonah know all about the workings of a solicitor's office, which would certainly be an advantage." He took another biscuit. "You know how much I value the *feel* of things, something you're very good at. Obviously the investigation proper is my job, but I won't deny you three could be very useful and I'd really value your input, dreadful word. Let's say your help."

"Well, of course, if we can . . ."

"Anyway," Roger said, looking at me quizzically, "what's happened to that famous curiosity of yours?"

"To be honest, Roger, when Thea was involved like that I was so angry I didn't have room for anything else!"

"But now?"

"Now? Well, I must admit that I have started to wonder . . ."

"That's what I want to hear!" He looked with faint surprise at the now empty biscuit plate and said hopefully, "There wouldn't be another cup of tea in the pot, would there?"

When Michael got home I told him what Roger had said.

"It makes sense, I suppose," Michael said thoughtfully. "We keep saying that Thea isn't going to get over this until the murderer is caught. So we might as well give it a go." He took my shopping-list pad and pencil down from the dresser and sat down at the kitchen table. "Now then, let's make some lists."

"If you remember we did try to work out where everyone was when it happened," I said, "and I think I still have a mental picture of that. Let's just make a list of the people and take each one as they come."

"Right. We'll start at the top. Hugh Barber."

"Well, he was out of the office, so it couldn't have been him."

"How do we know he was out of the office?"

"He rang from where he was with a client and asked Jackie to check something in a file."

"All right, fair enough. But we must get Jonah to check who the client was and if Hugh was there when he said he was—I mean, there might be some way he could have fiddled the times."

"That's a bit far-fetched, but okay."

Michael made a note on his list. "Right, then, what about Jason Chapman?"

"Well, he certainly *does* have a motive. We know that Gordon Masefield was probably having an affair with his wife."

"That's promising. But. . . ?"

"But, like Hugh, he was out of the office when it happened. Your discovery about the times on Gordon Masefield's computer clears him, as it did Thea."

"Yes, but you are Thea's alibi for the actual time of the murder and we don't know exactly *where* Jason Chapman was. I mean, was he with a client or what? That's another one for Jonah to check on. Anyway, it's different from Hugh—I mean Jason Chapman had a reason for killing Masefield, which Hugh doesn't seem to have had, and I'm definitely reluctant to lose anyone with a really good motive!"

"All right. Put him down with a query. So who else have we?"

"All the other people in the office."

"Ye-es," I said doubtfully. "I suppose so. But do you think we can find motives for them all. I mean, as we've said before, just disliking someone—and the wretched man was certainly disliked!—doesn't mean that you're going to kill him."

"True, but we might as well put them all on the list just in case. After all, we're still in the early stages, who knows *what* murky secrets we might discover."

"Well, there is Jackie, of course."

"Jackie?"

"Yes, one of the secretaries. I told you—Thea and I saw her with Gordon, so she might have been having an affair with him."

"You don't actually know that."

"Well, no, but from the way they were acting when we saw them in Exeter that day I don't think it was just a business lunch."

"Okay. But Jackie was with—what's the other girl's name?—with Carol at the time of the murder. And, anyway, if she was in love with him, poor sap, then she wouldn't be a likely suspect for his murder now, would she?"

"We don't know. He may have dumped her. Remember he was seen with Jason Chapman's wife *after* we saw him with Jackie."

"You think it might have been revenge? A bit far-fetched, surely! Besides, as I said, she was with the other girl right up to the time she went up and discovered the murder."

"I suppose so . . . no, wait a minute! How about if, after Hugh rang through and asked her to get the file from Gordon Masefield, she went up and found him a bit groggy after Thea had knocked him down and seized the opportunity to hit him over the head with the desk lamp?"

"Because he done her wrong?"

"Or because he'd stopped doing her wrong. Whatever. And then she screamed blue murder, as it were, as if she'd just found him."

"Ye-es," Michael said doubtfully. "Not really convincing, but I'll put it down anyway. Now what about the other girl, Carol?"

"No motive that we know of—unless Masefield was working his way systematically through all the female staff at Barber and Freeman. And Jackie is her alibi."

"Right. Clear sheet for Carol—as far as we know. Who else is there?"

"The girl in reception, Sally. She seems to have been pretty static, too. Just sitting there. And, again, no motive that we know of."

"Pity." Michael made another note on the pad. "Okay. Next?"

"There's Eileen Newton, she's the legal exec. You remember her, don't you. She used to work for your father."

"Oh yes, I think I do. Tall and thin and a bit intense. But she was always nice when I went to see Pa in the office and he was busy. She used to give me biscuits and ask about school. Yes, I remember her."

"Poor Eileen, she's had a lot of trouble. Her father's not been well and she's had to look after him as well as studying for her legal exec exams."

"So what do you think?"

"I saw her quite recently, actually, and she certainly didn't seem to like Gordon Masefield. She changed the subject quite abruptly when I mentioned him. In fact, come to think of it, she got up and left. But what's behind it all I really don't know."

"Aha! That sounds promising!"

"Michael! She's a really nice woman, not to mention being a regular churchgoer. I can't imagine her doing anything wrong."

"Who knows what people will do if they're under stress." Michael looked up from his notes. "Anyone else?"

"Well, there's Jonah," I said, "but I don't imagine you're going to include him!"

"No, not his style." Michael tore several sheets off the pad and put it back on the wall. "Right, then. What do we deduce from all that?"

I thought for a moment. "Not a lot. I mean, nothing actually springs to mind, does it?"

"No . . ." Michael looked rather downcast, then he said, "Of course, there's one thing we haven't considered."

"What's that?"

"Gordon Masefield himself. What do we know about him?"

"You're right. That's the way we should have approached things. So what *do* we know about him?"

"He's an off-comer, for a start. Well, he isn't, but his parents came to Taviscombe from somewhere else, I believe."

"Do we know where from?"

"No, but I'm sure with your information network you'll be able to find out something as simple as that."

"Are his parents still alive?" I asked, suddenly realizing that there might well be two people out there, people of my generation, mourning the death of a son.

"I think so. Oh yes, and he's got a brother, a bit younger than he is—was."

"Well, that's a start. Then, of course, there's poor little Wendy, and the child."

"And Wendy's parents and her brothers—the circle's widening by the minute."

"True. But," I objected, "it doesn't really help us, does it? I mean, even if any of these people had a motive for killing him, they still couldn't have got in without being seen by Carol or the other girls."

"Perhaps one of them *did* get in and either Carol or Jackie and Sally concealed the fact for some reason or other."

"It's not very likely, is it?" I said doubtfully.

"Not very likely, no, but *possible*. Come on, Ma, think positive!"

"All right, I'll try." I got up from the table. "Well, I'm going to have a glass of sherry before supper. I feel I've earned it. Let Foss in will you, darling, I can hear him bellowing outside the back door."

"Okay." Michael went toward the door. "And tomorrow you must get the Taviscombe mafia to work on the whole Masefield family. If anyone can find a skeleton in that cupboard, they can!"

Chapter Ten

It was quite obvious where I should start my investigations into the Masefield family. I telephoned Mrs. Dudley (one never just "dropped in" on her) and was invited to lunch. The fact that it was lunch rather than tea was significant. Tea was for the younger generation—Rosemary's friends and contemporaries and also for the lesser members of her acquaintance. Lunch, however, was for her own contemporaries or for those whom she had known and approved of (by no means the same thing) for a sufficient number of years (at least thirty), for them to have achieved a sort of honorary contemporaneity. It marked a considerable advance in our relationship.

Remembering the hothouse temperature at which the aged always keep their houses, I wore the lightest of my summer dresses and I took with me the usual tribute of a large and expensive arrangement of flowers.

"Come in, come in, Sheila, don't stand about in the doorway! Come in and sit down." Her voice was as strong as ever, though the hand that motioned me to a chair trembled slightly. I laid the flowers on a small table beside her and her expression softened.

"Thank you Sheila, they are very nice." She picked up the bouquet and held it up to her face. "It is perfectly ridiculous that carnations nowadays have no *smell*," she said, reverting to her usual acerbic manner. "I cannot understand it. Where did you buy them, was it Ascott's?" I nodded. "I shall certainly have a word with them when I am in there next!"

She seemed disposed to continue on this theme but fortunately Elsie, her slave of all work, came in bearing a small silver tray on which were two glasses.

"The sherry for Mrs. Malory, Elsie, and I will have my usual brandy. I assume you drink Tio Pepe, Sheila?"

"Lovely," I murmured dutifully as I took the delicate glass, though, to be honest, I would rather have had an Amontillado.

"Dr. Waterman insists that I have a glass of brandy every day," Mrs. Dudley said. "He says that it is essential to my health. It is the only thing that keeps me going."

Since Mrs. Dudley had taken a small glass of brandy every day for the last twenty years, to my certain knowledge, I didn't pay too much attention to this remark, though I did note, in passing, that she had obviously changed her doctor yet again.

"Well, now." Mrs. Dudley laid her glass down

and regarded me sharply. "What is all this about that young woman of Michael's?"

I braced myself to face a hostile inquisition, forgetting for the moment that she had a soft spot for Michael.

"It was an absolute *disgrace*," she continued. "I've told Rosemary that I intend writing to the chief constable about it. His father was an old friend of my late husband, you know, so he always listens to me. It would be a complete travesty if *that man* was allowed to get away with such an appalling miscarriage of justice!"

"It was very distressing . . ." I began, but Mrs. Dudley, who obviously didn't want to hear my opinion of the matter, went on.

"I have, of course, made my views known to Roger, but it is essential that something should be done by the *highest* authority."

"Actually," I ventured, "I don't think Thea wants to make a fuss about it. I think she just wants to put it all behind her."

"*Nonsense!* That would be quite wrong! She seems to be a sensible girl, from what I've seen of her (though the less said the better about that idiotic father of hers—fancy being caught by that common little Glynis Williams!) and I cannot believe that she would be so poor-spirited as to let that dreadful Bridges man get off scot-free."

I knew better than to contradict Mrs. Dudley when she was in full flow and I just hoped that Thea's path would not cross hers in the immediate future.

"Of course," Mrs. Dudley said as she moved slowly and painfully into the dining room, "I always said it was a great mistake for Roger to go traipsing about in America. I said to him, 'What on earth do you imagine you can learn from a lot of gangsters?' and I was right, you see. The moment he was gone something like this happened. Roger may be young and headstrong like all young people, but he would never have done such a foolish thing as arresting Thea, a girl of good family and engaged to a very respectable young man." I treasured the phrase to repeat to Michael and made affirming noises. "Yes, I certainly intend to do something about it. I think I may say I still stand for something in this town."

She sat down firmly in the high carver chair at the head of the table and motioned me to take my place beside her. Elsie had prepared a marvelous lunch of salmon mayonnaise and asparagus and I was hoping to enjoy it in relative peace when Mrs. Dudley began again.

"I can't say I was surprised when I heard about that Gordon Masefield," she said.

Since this was what I had come to hear I raised my head from a pleased contemplation of my plate and looked at her enquiringly.

"Well, you only have to look at his family to see that he would come to a bad end."

"Really? What are they like, then?"

Mrs. Dudley maneuvered a spear of asparagus carefully into her mouth before embarking on one of her expositions of Taviscombe life and history.

"The family came here in the war, evacuees from Birmingham. *He,* that is Eric Masefield, the father, had some sort of factory there and he sent his wife and children here to be out of the way of the bombing."

"How many children were there?"

"Only two, a boy and a girl, both in their teens. The boy went off to join the army and the girl married Ted Hopkins—do you remember him? He had a hill farm, a very poor sort of place, out beyond Hawkridge. Her father forbade the marriage, but the mother encouraged her and she was a very headstrong girl. In the end the pair ran off together and got married in a registry office in Taunton—a very hole-and-corner affair. She died quite young, I believe, and there were no children."

"How sad."

Mrs. Dudley gave a little snort of contempt. "Foolish, more like. Anyway, after the war Eric Masefield retired to Taviscombe—his wife didn't want to move back to Birmingham, and who can blame her! He sold the factory (and got a very good price for it, from what I heard) and they bought that big house on West Hill that used to belong to the Frobishers. When the son, Roy, came back from the war he wanted to stay down here, too, so his father set him up in a farm machinery business—Taviscombe Machinery."

"Oh, is that who owns it? I never knew."

"He did very nicely, well, you know how many branches there are now. And then, when Eric Masefield died, there was all his money, too. Oh, Roy Masefield was quite a catch!"

"So who caught him?"

"Do you remember the Clarendons who lived out at North Lynch? She was distantly related to Lord Babbacombe—a very good family, but poor as church mice. Their youngest daughter, Harriet, she married Roy Masefield."

Mrs. Dudley wiped her lips with her table napkin and rang the small bell beside her plate.

It's always something of a shock when someone appears at the ring of a bell—extraordinary, really, to think how things have changed in such a short time. I can perfectly well remember as a child my mother pressing a bell in the drawing room that summoned our maid Louie from the kitchen, but now it seems not just another age, but another world.

"That was *delicious*, Elsie," I said as the little figure removed the plates.

"I made a queen of puddings, Miss Sheila," Elsie said. "I remembered how much you liked them as a little girl."

"Oh, Elsie, how lovely! I can never get the meringue right, it always sinks into the custard. And I do love it so!"

"The Clarendons," Mrs. Dudley continued, ignoring this little interchange, "were quite pleased with the match—well, it did mean that *one* of the girls was settled. The other two never married. One of them stayed at home and the other went off with a friend to breed dogs—I think it was dogs, but might have been cats—something like that, anyway. Daphne, that was the girl who stayed with her parents, had a nervous breakdown, or that's what they *called* it, and ended up in some sort of Home in Torquay—or was it Paignton? My memory isn't what it was."

"Goodness! I never knew all this."

"Roy and Harriet Masefield," Mrs. Dudley said, helping herself lavishly to clotted cream, something forbidden her surely, even by a new doctor, "had two sons—Gordon, he was the eldest, and Donald. I suppose," she added, going to the nub of the matter as always, "it will be Donald who will inherit all the money now."

I spooned a rather smaller amount of cream onto my pudding. "The money?" I enquired.

"Oh yes, there will be quite a fortune. Roy must be worth a great deal in his own right, and then there was the grandfather's money as well. Oh yes, young Donald will be well set up."

"But Gordon had a wife and child," I protested.

"It was a girl," Mrs. Dudley said dismissively. "She certainly wouldn't inherit the business."

I didn't comment on this blatantly sexist remark, knowing from experience that it would be useless to do so, but I made a mental note to check on the situation if it was at all possible.

"What's Donald like?" I asked.

"A poor creature," Mrs. Dudley said dismissively. "Couldn't say boo to a goose. No, Roy Masefield will be very upset, he doted on Gordon—a chip off the old block, you might say."

"In what way?"

"Roy was very ambitious and quite ruthless in business, and I've heard that Gordon was much the same in his own line."

"Yes, I think that's true. At least, that's the impression I've got from Michael and Jonah."

"Exactly," Mrs. Dudley said with satisfaction. "And there were other things, too," she added darkly.

"You mean—women?" I enquired.

"Certainly." She lowered her voice, as she always did when about to pass on some particularly choice piece of gossip, so that I had to strain to hear her. "There was a great deal of talk about Roy Masefield and Cecily Barker. In fact, from what I hear, that last child wasn't Dennis Barker's at all!"

"Really?"

"Oh yes. Then there was that business with Alice Silkin."

I spooned up the last of my delicious pudding and concentrated. "What was that?"

"Alice Silkin was a widow whose husband had built up a very nice light engineering business over Exebridge way. Roy Masefield made up to her—she was a poor little thing and easily flattered, I believe—and the long and the short of it was she sold him the business for a fraction of what it was worth."

"Goodness!"

"Her son was furious. But he was away in Australia when all this happened and when he got back it was all over. The business had been left to her, you see. Such a mistake. Women are not really suited to such things."

It has never ceased to amaze me how Mrs. Dudley manages to reconcile these anti-feminist views with the fact that she dominated her poor husband, both at home and in his business (he was an accountant) throughout his short life. But then, consistency has never meant a great deal to her. "Anyway, as I was saying, Roy Masefield has always had a very bad reputation where women are concerned, and it seems that Gordon has followed in his father's footsteps."

"Really?"

"Oh yes," Mrs. Dudley said firmly, "it's common knowledge."

"He has got a wife," I suggested.

Mrs. Dudley gave a snort of contempt. "That little Wendy Lewis! Well, of course, the Masefields were furious about that—at least Roy was. I don't suppose *she* has much of an opinion about anything. He wanted a much grander marriage for his son! No, Gordon Masefield wouldn't have married her except for the fact that her father made him. Well"—the voice was lowered again—"there was a baby on the way and Keith Lewis could have made a great deal of trouble for the Masefields, since he is on the district council's planning committee and they have these expansion plans for the business, you know."

"No," I said, marveling as I always did at Mrs. Dudley's positively encyclopedic knowledge of *everything* that went on in Taviscombe, "I didn't know."

Mrs. Dudley looked faintly surprised at my ignorance and went on, "I believe the Masefields wanted her to get rid of the baby, but of course they didn't dare say so openly since the Lewises are Catholics and very devout."

Why, I wondered idly, were Catholics, more than other religions, always credited with this special devoutness. Were there no devout Methodists, or Buddhists for that matter?

"I see," I said.

"Oh, Gordon Masefield has a *dreadful* reputation," Mrs. Dudley said with some satisfaction. "Perfectly dreadful."

"Yes," I said, "I had heard." Elsie came in to clear the table and I got up. "I must go and let you go and have your afternoon rest. Thank you so much for a delicious lunch and for a lovely visit."

Her face softened momentarily. "It is very good of you," she said, "to spare time for an old woman. Young people nowadays are always so *busy*."

I felt a pang of guilt, remembering my reason for coming. Mrs. Dudley slowly got to her feet and on an impulse I went over and hugged her.

"Good-bye," I said. "I'll come again soon."

She gave me what Rosemary calls her Brave Smile. "I will always be pleased to see you, Sheila, for as long as I'm Spared." With that she made the sort of exit that Mrs. Siddons might have envied and left me feeling, as I always do after such an encounter, an absolute worm.

Chapter Eleven

I had so much to think about when I got home that I hardly knew where to begin. Such richness! So many more motives for Gordon Masefield's death.

"Masses more potential suspects," I told Michael when he got home. "There's the brother Donald, for a start—money, after all is the prime reason for murder, and I'd no idea that there was so *much* money! Then there's all Wendy Lewis's family— they can hardly be pleased with the way Gordon treated her. There's the father and several brothers, I believe . . ."

Michael smiled at my enthusiasm. "There's just one thing you've forgotten," he said. "How did they get past reception?"

"Oh," I said impatiently, "I'm sure we'll find a way round that! No, we must somehow get to know the Masefields. I know them by sight, of course, but not really to speak to. Then I'll be able to see if I think any of them are murderers."

"Just like that?" Michael laughed.

"Well," I said, "I'll certainly have *some* idea of the sort of people they are."

My opportunity to meet Roy Masefield came sooner than I expected, though it was not a pleasant encounter. Laura Richardson was giving what she called her annual Bash, not something I usually looked forward to. Crowded with too many people in a not-very-large room, clutching a glass of warm white wine in one hand and a rock-hard bit of toast with what Michael calls bits of minced-up fish on it in the other, with my handbag strap slipping inexorably from my shoulder, I wondered why on earth I hadn't thought of some convincing reason not to come. But I was fond of Laura and I decided I needn't stay long.

"Hello. You got roped in, too?" It was Rosemary at my elbow. "I cannot imagine how so many people can *breathe* in such a confined space!"

"I know, it is pretty squashy, isn't it? I'm just calculating how soon I can slip away without causing offense."

"I've only just got here, so I'll have to stay for a bit. Jack, needless to say, has a convenient committee meeting. Let's move over to the other end of the room, there seems to be a bit more space over there."

As we edged our way cautiously through the crowded room, I could hear, even above the roar of general conversation, one voice raised very loudly.

"It's a bloody disgrace! It's . . ." The voice stumbled and hesitated as if the owner was not quite sober. "It's undue influence!" The words were brought out triumphantly. "That's what it is."

"Oh Lord," Rosemary said. "It's Roy Masefield

sounding off about something, and he seems to be pretty drunk. Poor Laura! *Not* the best way to make a party a success!"

I looked curiously at the man in the corner who had buttonholed poor Jane Cardus, who was obviously deeply embarrassed by the situation.

Roy Masefield is a tall, thickset man with the remains of the sort of flashy good looks that his son Gordon had. But where Gordon had been insinuating, and, with women especially, with a sort of specious charm, Roy's manner was more aggressive and what he probably thought of as masterful and authoritative.

"It's a disgrace!" he repeated. "That bloody woman kills my son and she gets off scot-free! And all because she knows the bloody local police! They had her in prison, they knew she did it—but no, when Chief Inspector bloody Eliot comes back she's let out, isn't she? Don't tell me *that* wasn't influence . . ."

Furious, I instinctively moved forward to confront him, but Rosemary laid a hand on my arm.

"Leave it," she said. "He's drunk. Nobody's taking any notice of him."

As she spoke I saw Keith Richardson, Laura's husband, moving across the room. He took Roy Masefield's arm and said something quietly in his ear. Masefield shook him off angrily, but eventually allowed himself to be led into another room.

"Come on," Rosemary said briskly. "Let's get out of here. Come home with me and we'll have a proper drink in peace."

* * *

"There now." Rosemary put a cold, frosted glass in my hand. "That's better. There's something about party wine, if you know what I mean. It can be the best Chardonnay, Merlot, or whatever, (and I'm sure Laura only has the best!) but when it's dished out in bulk it becomes completely tasteless. Have you noticed?"

I took a sip of my gin and tonic and smiled gratefully. "Thanks," I said. "I really needed that!"

"You mustn't worry about Roy Masefield," Rosemary said, pushing Alpha, her boxer, to one side of the sofa and sitting down. "He was so obviously drunk!"

"I know he was. But I was so *furious*! I mean, he's probably been going around Taviscombe saying things like that about Thea even when he's sober."

"The thing is," Rosemary said, "he's lost a son whom he adored and he's looking around for someone to blame and he doesn't much care who."

"Yes, you're right. I suppose I should feel sorry for him. Well, I am, really, of course I am. It's a dreadful thing to happen—the worst thing that can happen to anyone, to lose a child. It's just that I can't bear it if he goes around spreading lies about Thea. Poor girl, she's had quite enough to put up with without that!"

"How is she now?" Rosemary asked.

"Better, I think. The kitten helped. She still hasn't gone back to work, though."

"It'll take time."

"I'm afraid it will," I agreed. "Michael does try to

understand and to be sensitive about it, but I don't suppose we'll any of us ever know quite how awful it was for her. She still won't talk about it."

"It would help if she could."

"Apparently they suggested counseling, but she wouldn't."

"No, well I can understand that. What about Mr. Whittaker?"

"The vicar? No, I don't think so. Thea's never been a regular churchgoer, and, anyway, to be quite honest, I don't see myself pouring my heart out to *him*, do you?"

"Not really." Rosemary got up and took my glass. "Will you have another?"

"I'd better not if I've got to drive myself home. Anyway, I feel perfectly well comforted now."

"Well, stay and keep me company over supper. It's only cold because Jack's out and I don't bother to cook for myself."

"I wonder if I'll cook when it's just me?" I said thoughtfully. "When Michael's married, I mean. I expect I will, though, because I'm so greedy! Yes please, I'd love to stay."

"Roy Masefield's a peculiar man," Rosemary said as she carved the cold beef. "He's very moody. He can be quite pleasant, then he suddenly gets all het up and angry over the smallest things. Poor Harriet, I can't imagine how she puts up with it!"

"Do you know her?"

"Only slightly; we were on that Aid to the Sudan committee together. Though I think she was only there because they wanted a big subscription from *him*—she hardly opened her mouth! I used to know her sister, not Daphne, the middle one, Jennifer. You remember her, don't you? A big girl, rather lumpy, in saggy tweed skirts and bitten-off hair. She met this formidable woman at the Bath and West and eventually went off to breed dogs with her somewhere on the south coast. Harriet was always the quiet one. I think she was rather flattered when Roy paid her attention."

"I wonder how she's taking Gordon's death?"

"I don't know. Actually, I think Donald's her favorite. Certainly he's more like her. He keeps that secondhand bookshop in Dunster. You know the one, off the main street up beyond the church."

"I'd have thought Roy Masefield would want at least one of his sons to work in the firm."

"He did," Rosemary said, hacking pieces off a loaf of crusty bread. "Here, sorry it's so crumbly, but it's very new. No, Donald did go into the firm straight from school but, from what I can gather he was pretty hopeless—no drive, no initiative, none of the things that Roy Masefield wanted. I think he was pretty unpleasant to the poor boy, but eventually he decided to cut his losses and bought him the lease of this bookshop."

"Oh dear. So what about Gordon? Why didn't he go into the business?"

"Oh, Roy's a bit of a snob and he quite liked having a son in one of the professions. To be honest, I think he knew that he and Gordon were too alike not to have clashed over how to run things. I expect he assumed that when he retired Gordon would take over. He's more or less washed his hands of Donald."

"Another reason for feeling so bitter about Gordon's death," I said. "So Wendy's little girl will probably inherit everything now."

"Yes, poor child."

"Poor child?"

"Well, yes, just think how Roy Masefield will want to supervise her upbringing, so that she turns out the sort of person *he* wants her to be. Wendy's such a little mouse she won't dare to oppose him!"

"No, I suppose not." I cut a little of the cheese that Rosemary pushed toward me. "This is delicious Brie, just runny enough. I wonder how Gordon and Donald got on?"

"Oh, Gordon despised him, of course. Poor Harriet did tell me, in a burst of confidence, how she wished Gordon wouldn't always pick on Donald when they met. Actually, from what she implied, I think Donald was rather keen on Wendy until Gordon stepped in. Apparently they'd been going out together, but then I suppose Gordon couldn't resist taking her off his little brother, although I don't think he particularly wanted her for himself."

"How ghastly!"

"Well, Gordon was ghastly. I think Harriet positively disliked him in the end. It's quite clear that Donald was her favorite—because he was so like her, I expect, just as Gordon took after Roy."

*   *   *

"So you see," I said to Michael, "Donald had another reason for killing his brother, as well as the money."

"Yes, I suppose so," Michael said doubtfully. "But from what you say, Donald doesn't sound like a murderer to me."

"You never know. People can be pushed too far. 'Even a worm will turn if it's trod on,' as old Mrs. Carpenter used to say. Perhaps the Wendy thing was a step too far for Donald. And then there's Harriet, too. *She* might have done it."

"Oh, come on, Ma. Infanticide?"

"Gordon wasn't an infant!"

"You know what I mean. 'Can a mother's loving care fail toward the child she bear,' and all that."

"Oh, Rosemary and I always used to giggle in assembly about the child she-bear!" I exclaimed irrelevantly. "No, really, I'm sure she feels so protective about Donald because he's her ewe lamb and Gordon was persecuting him."

"All these worms and lambs and bears," Michael said. "It's like a menagerie! Talking of which, that wretched kitten you gave to Thea has lacerated my leg—it seems to think I'm a climbing frame or something. And Thea just smiles and says, 'Oh, isn't she sweet!'"

"Well, I'm glad she's smiling about something," I said.

"Oh, yes, I knew there was something. She's given me some papers to take into the office. I can't do it tomorrow, I'm afraid, because I've got to go and see a client's accountant, so could you?"

"Yes, of course."

"If you could give them to Jonah. Thanks, Ma."

"I've got to go in to the shops anyway. Now, do go up to the bathroom and put some disinfectant on those kitten scratches."

When I got to Barber and Freeman Sally, the receptionist, said that Jonah was busy and would I like to wait. I suppose I could have just left the papers, but I was glad to have an opportunity to look over the scene of the crime, as it were, so I said I'd wait.

"Would you like a cup of coffee, Mrs. Malory?" Sally asked.

"Thank you, that would be lovely," I said.

"Why don't you go and sit at the back with Carol," she said. "It's more comfortable there."

She disappeared behind a door marked STAFF and I went through the reception area and into the large open office at the back where the two secretaries worked.

Carol was sitting at her word processer but there was no sign of Jackie. I knew Carol slightly because of cricket teas—her current boyfriend was on the team.

"Hello, Carol," I said, "how are you?"

"Oh, hello, Mrs. Malory. I'm fine, though I'm a bit busy with Jackie away."

"Oh dear, is she ill?"

Carol hesitated. "Not ill exactly."

"I expect she's still suffering from the shock of

finding Gordon Masefield's body," I suggested, "especially since . . ." I broke off.

Carol looked at me questioningly. "Especially since?" she asked.

"Oh dear, you'll think me a dreadful gossip, but I did see her with Gordon in Exeter once. They seemed, well, very close. So I thought—if she was involved with him in some way—she would have been particularly upset at finding him like that."

"Oh, she was!" Carol burst out. "It was really awful!" She broke off as Sally came into the room with a cup of coffee.

"There you are, Mrs. Malory," Sally said. "Sorry to keep you waiting. He won't be long now."

There was a moment's silence after Sally had gone away, as if Carol was trying to decide whether to say anything else. I stirred my coffee in what I hoped was an encouraging manner and waited. After a while Carol said, "Do you mind if I tell you something in confidence? Only there's no one else I can tell. I mean, I did promise Jackie I wouldn't, but since you saw them together you've probably guessed . . ."

"That they were having an affair?" I asked. "Yes, well, it did look rather like an office romance."

"It was more than that," Carol said, "at least on Jackie's side. She really thought he was going to divorce that dim wife of his and marry her. As if!"

"From what I know of Gordon Masefield it doesn't seem very likely," I said.

"That's what I kept telling her, but the stupid idiot was absolutely besotted. He bought her presents and took her out to nightclubs in Exeter and Plymouth. They even went for a couple of weekends to London, and she thought it was all the big time. Then, of course, it happened."

"What happ . . . Oh dear, do you mean she got pregnant?"

"Yes, she did. If you ask me she did it deliberately, thinking he'd *have* to marry her. I mean, we all know that's why he married Wendy."

"Yes, but Wendy's father had something that Gordon's father wanted," I said. "I don't suppose Jackie was in that sort of position?"

"Too right!"

"So how did Gordon react when Jackie told him? I assume she did tell him?"

"Oh yes, couldn't wait! No, he was furious."

"Oh dear."

"He told her she'd have to get rid of it."

"Poor girl!"

"She was very upset. Well, you would be, wouldn't you? I mean, she was a fool, but she really did love him."

"So what happened then?"

"She said she wouldn't and that made him more furious than ever. He turned really nasty, even accused her of blackmailing him for money, and she never ever did that!"

"How long ago was all this?"

"About three months ago."

"Has Jackie told her parents?"

"No, she's really scared of her stepfather, and her mother's not much use; she's scared of him, too."

"So you're the only person who knows about it—now that Gordon Masefield's dead, that is."

"Yes. It's a bit awkward really, because she's not been very well, a lot of sickness and so on, and she keeps on having to have time off. She says it's a stomach bug, but Mr. Chapman is getting a bit fed up about it."

"Poor Jackie! So it really must have upset her to find Gordon like that."

"Oh, it did. She'd been sick earlier that day—a couple of times, actually, and I'd had to cover for her—so you can imagine how it was when *that* happened!"

"How dreadful."

"She'd sort of worked herself up into hating him, I think, because he'd been so horrible to her, but then, when he was dead, well . . ."

"Yes, I do see. So what is she going to do now?"

"She doesn't know and *I* don't know what to tell her. I mean, Mrs. Malory, it's very awkward for me. It's not as if we're real friends or anything, we just work together, but she's sort of come to rely on me and I honestly don't want the responsibility . . ." She broke off. "That sounds really mean, doesn't it? But I just don't know *what* to say to her!" She looked at me hopefully, as if I might provide some magic solution to the problem. "Actually," she went on, "it's been really good to be able to tell someone else."

"Yes, well," I said, "it does seem hard that you should be burdened with all this. Are you sure she can't tell her mother? That really would be the best solution."

"No. I've *told* her lots of times, but she says she daren't."

"And she still wants to keep the baby?"

"Oh yes."

"Then perhaps she'd better tell Gordon's mother. Not his father, he'd be quite unsympathetic, but Harriet Masefield might be able to help in some way. It's worth a try."

"I'll tell her. To be honest, Mrs. Malory, I've been really worried that she might do something silly— you know—so anything that would stop her . . ."

The door opened and Sally came into the room.

"He's free now, Mrs. Malory, if you'd like to come this way."

As I got up to go I said to Carol, "Do let me know how things turn out," and followed Sally upstairs to Jonah's office.

We took the back stairs leading up from the corridor outside the secretaries' room and, as we went, something suddenly occurred to me. If Carol was looking after Jackie while she was being sick in the Ladies, then anyone could have come in by the back door and gone up to Gordon Masefield's office without being seen. Neither of the girls would have told the police—or, indeed, anyone else—that they hadn't been in their office for some part of the afternoon. The field was wide open for any of the new suspects from outside the office. Practically *anyone* could have killed Gordon Masefield.

Chapter Twelve

I gave Jonah the files from Thea. I think he was rather surprised that I hadn't just handed them in, but had waited to see him in person.

"Do you have a moment?" I asked.

"Yes, I'm free until twelve. Is there something?"

"Well, actually I've been wanting to have a look round here and this did seem to be a good opportunity. It isn't just ghoulish curiosity, it's just that if I am going to try and help solve this wretched murder I thought I really ought to see the scene of the crime, as it were."

"Sure. No problem. Good idea." He got up and led the way out into the corridor where he opened a door and said, "This was Gordon's room." He stood aside for me to go in.

It was a fair-sized room, with a large desk, two chairs, and several filing cabinets. The desk was empty except for a telephone and the computer that had meant so much to Thea. The lamp, since it was the murder weapon, was presumably still with the police. There was a lighter patch on the carpet. Jonah saw me looking at it.

"Blood," he said. "The police said we could have it cleaned after they'd finished in here, but I think we'll have to get a new one."

I shuddered. "Yes, I think you should."

The room, which had seemed so ordinary and prosaic when I first entered it, suddenly felt strange and threatening. I turned to go.

"Thanks, Jonah," I said. "I hardly know what I expected to find."

We went back into the corridor. "This is Hugh's room," Jonah said, opening another door.

Hugh, as befitted the senior partner, had a large room, book-lined and imposing. His desk, unlike Gordon's light, modern one, was heavy mahogany, embellished with tooled leather. The chairs were leather, too, and the long curtains at the large bay window were of heavy brocade.

"Very impressive," I said, looking round. "Hugh was out, wasn't he, when it happened?"

"Yes, he was with old Walter Meredith."

"Really? I know him quite well, he was a friend of my mother's."

"The police checked with him, of course, and Hugh was there. Not that anyone would suspect Hugh!"

"Not really. When's he due back? Have you heard from him?"

"About another ten days, I think. Actually, it's really very awkward him being away now. I mean, with Gordon gone and Thea not here . . ."

"Mr. Chapman has been very good about Thea, but I do see how shorthanded you must be."

"Eileen Newton has been marvelous, we've given her quite a lot of extra stuff to do, but it's not the same, of course."

We went out of Hugh's room back into the corridor.

"Is this the closed file room?" I asked, indicating an open door.

"Yes. Do you want to see that?" Jonah pushed the door further open and we went in. It was a large room almost entirely filled with filing cabinets, some modern metal ones but some, in an alcove, were very old wooden ones, several stacked on top of each other so that they formed a rather dangerous looking tower. Because some of the cabinets were pushed up against the window the room was dark and had that indefinable smell of dust and paper and possibly dead mice that such places do have.

"Goodness," I said. "What a lot of files!"

"Yes, it's ridiculous," Jonah said. "We should get all the back stuff onto computer and have a really good clear-out here. But, of course, no one's got the time, so it just stays here and we still rummage about in those ghastly files for things. So much for progress!"

We went out onto the landing again.

"Well," I said, "I mustn't take up any more of your time. Thank you so much, Jonah, for letting me look around."

"My pleasure. I just wish there was some way we could get this wretched business cleared up. I can quite understand why Thea finds it so difficult to come back. We're all looking over our shoulder a bit, wondering just *who* the guilty one might be!"

For a moment I thought of telling Jonah about the possibility of other suspects from outside the office, but since Carol had told me about Jackie in confidence I didn't feel I could. Not that Jackie would be able to keep her secret for that much longer. Still, until that moment came I knew I couldn't be the one to tell Jonah.

There was someone I felt I could tell, though. When I got home I rang Thea.

"Can I come and see you this afternoon?" I asked. "Or don't you feel like visitors?"

"No, please do come. Come to tea—I'll make a cake!"

It was a very nice cake, a Victoria sandwich filled with raspberry jam and dusted with icing sugar.

"It's lovely!" I told Thea as I took the first bite. "Beautifully light and just slightly chewy—a perfect texture!"

Thea laughed. "Thank goodness! I was very apprehensive, you're such an expert!"

"It is true," I said judicially, "that I am very widely experienced in the matter of Victoria sponges. No one who has presided over as many produce stalls at bring-and-buy sales as I have could hardly fail to be experienced in such matters. However," I went on, taking another bite, "in the actual *manufacture* of sponges, Victorian and otherwise, I am by no means infallible—you ask Rosemary, she's seen too many of my half-risen, lop-sided creations!"

Thea laughed. "I don't believe a word of it! Anyway, I'm glad it's all right. I enjoyed cooking again. It really is very therapeutic. I made some brownies for Michael because he does love them so." She sighed. "Poor Michael, he's been so good and patient with me. I feel really guilty . . ."

"My dear Thea," I broke in, "you mustn't talk like that. You've had a dreadful experience and we all know—and no one better than Michael—that it's going to take you a long time to come to terms with it. So, please, no more nonsense about feeling guilty."

"Actually," Thea said, "I've been thinking, I really ought to be getting back to work. They must be very short-staffed, with Hugh away and . . ."

"Yes," I said hastily. "I was talking to Jonah yesterday, when I took him those files you sent, and he said how busy they were. But honestly, no one's going to put any pressure on you to go back until you feel really ready." I hesitated for a moment and then I went on, "I had quite a chat with Carol while I was waiting for Jonah to be free and she told me something very interesting."

"Really?"

"She told me that Jackie's pregnant and it seems likely that at the relevant time that afternoon—after you'd gone—they weren't in their room, but in the loo where poor Jackie was being sick."

"So you mean. . . ?"

"That anyone—anyone at all from outside—

could have come in the back way and gone up the back stairs and murdered Gordon Masefield. The murderer doesn't have to be someone in the office after all!"

"Good heavens!" Thea exclaimed. "And poor Jackie! I suppose the baby was Gordon's—there was that time we saw them in Exeter, and then, in the office after that, I felt there was something quite heavy going on. Poor girl, she must be dreadfully upset!"

"Yes. But he wanted her to get rid of the baby and was absolutely vile to her when she wouldn't, so I think, by the time he died, she'd actually come to hate him."

"Hate him enough to. . . ?"

"To kill him? I don't know. She was pretty desperate, though. Apparently she's got absolutely no one to turn to. According to Carol she has an unpleasant stepfather and a mother who's terrified of him. So if Gordon failed her, who knows what she might have done? I've never met her—what is she like, as a person, I mean?"

Thea hesitated. "I honestly don't know. There seems to be the most tremendous gap between her generation and mine," she said.

"Really?"

"Oh yes. Fashions change so quickly, not just in clothes and music and so forth. Now that I'm practically a thirty-something, I really don't know what girls in their late teens think and feel about anything. Mind you, being pregnant and having no one to support you must be pretty dreadful at any age. And you say no one knows?"

"Only Carol and, although she seems to me to be a sensible girl, she really doesn't want to get involved. They don't seem to be friends. In fact, I got the impression that Carol strongly disapproved of the whole affair."

"As well she might!" Thea exclaimed. "The entire office knew what sort of person Gordon was. Still," she went on, "I suppose when you're as young and impressionable as Jackie, you don't take any notice of what other people say. She may even have thought that she could change him."

As we both sat considering this thought, a small furry creature erupted into the room and began to claw my chair.

"Wicked one," Thea said, carefully unhooking the kitten and placing it on my lap.

"Hasn't she grown!" I said, stroking the long fur and trying, not entirely successfully, to avoid the needle-sharp teeth and claws. "She's certainly very playful!" The kitten pounced on my hand and kicked it with her small back feet so I picked her up and held her in the air away from me. She batted perfunctorily at my hair with her paw and then gave a great yawn and, when I put her back onto my lap, curled up, her nose buried in her tail, and promptly fell asleep.

"I wish I could do that," Thea said, "fall asleep like that!"

"Have you been having bad nights?" I asked.

"It's better now, but it wasn't very good at first. I

had these nightmares . . ." She sat quietly for a while, her hands folded in her lap, looking out of the window at the stretch of beach and the sea below. Then she smiled and said, "But that's all over now. In fact I think I'll go back to work on Monday."

"Oh, Thea, that's splendid! I'm sure, once you've got over the first half hour, it will be so much better for you to be fully occupied again. And, from what Jonah said, you'll be welcomed back with open arms."

Thea did go back to work and life went on, the days passing so much more quickly than they used to, so that soon we were suddenly at the end of the summer without my having done half the things I'd meant to do.

"It's the last match of the season," Michael said. "Can you help with the teas?"

"Yes, I suppose so. That is, if someone else can look after the urn."

"Thea said she'd make some little cakes."

"That was nice of her. At least, she knows what she's getting into, marrying you—endless cricket teas stretching into infinity!"

"Oh, she doesn't mind," Michael said. "Anyway, she offered."

After what had been a particularly wet season, Fate relented and Saturday was one of those perfect early autumn days when the sun still has warmth in it and the sky is that wonderful almost Mediterranean blue.

When I went into the little kitchen at the back of the pavilion I found Carol there, instead of Monica, as I'd expected.

"Hello," I said, "did they rope you in, too?"

"Oh, Keith said that the lady who was going to help had a cold so could I do it instead."

"That's very noble of you."

"Well, I was coming anyway, so it's no bother. Actually, Mrs. Malory, I think cricket's a bit boring. I only come because Keith gets hurt if I don't, you know how they are! I'd just as soon be in here doing the sandwiches."

I smiled and began taking various things from my shopping bag.

"There's a couple of fruitcakes and a chocolate cake and here's the ham for the sandwiches and the bread. Thea, Miss Wyatt, is bringing some scones and jam and some small cakes as well. I think that should be enough."

Carol began putting things onto plates. "I was so glad when Miss Wyatt came back to the office. It must have been really awful for her, what happened. I don't think I could have ever faced the place again!"

"No, it was quite an effort for her, I think. Still, I'm sure it was for the best. It's always a good thing to exorcise our ghosts."

"Mrs. Malory." Carol stopped buttering the sliced loaf and stood with her knife suspended in the air. "Mrs. Malory," she began again and stopped as if she didn't know how to go on.

"Yes?" I said encouragingly.

"You know what I told you about Jackie? About her being—you know—"

"Yes."

"Well, can you please forget that I told you?"

"Yes, of course."

There was a pause while Carol was apparently deciding what to tell me, then she went on. "Actually, she's had a miscarriage."

"Oh, poor girl! When did it happen?"

"Last Saturday. She was out with some friends at a club in Exeter."

"How awful!"

"Well, fortunately one of the girls she was with got her to hospital, so she's all right."

I shook my head. "It must have been terrible for her."

"She said it was pretty horrible, in the toilets like that. And then waiting for the ambulance with everybody knowing . . ."

"And she's really all right?"

"Yes, she didn't come in to work on Monday or Tuesday but she's back now."

"What about her parents?"

"Oh, they don't know. She got this girl to ring and say that she was staying with her overnight."

"I see."

"So you see, no one in Taviscombe knows, and Jackie doesn't know that I've told you."

"No. I quite understand. But poor girl, what a dreadful thing to have happened."

Carol began to cut one of the fruitcakes carefully into slices. "Well, I don't know. It's probably for the best—well, that's what I think. It would have been ever so complicated for her, what with her parents and everything. No, she's much better off the way things turned out."

"And do you think Jackie feels like that?"

Carol shrugged. "I don't know really. I can't make her out. She seems angry more than anything."

"Angry?"

"Yes, when she told me she kept on saying, 'It was all for nothing.' It seemed a funny sort of thing to say after something like that happening. What do you think she meant?"

I unwound some cling-film and wrapped it round one of the plates of sandwiches.

"I don't know. I suppose she was thinking of all the miseries of being sick and worrying about her parents and so on."

"Yes, I suppose so," Carol said doubtfully. "But it didn't *sound* as if that was what she meant." She put the last of the sliced fruitcake on a plate. "Well now, do you want me to see to the urn, Mrs. Malory?"

"Oh, would you? I'm hopeless with the wretched thing. It seems to know I'm afraid of it!"

Carol gave me a perfunctory little smile, as if acknowledging a joke she didn't see the point of.

"Oh, that's all right. They've got one like this at the Methodist Church Hall."

"Well, I'll just go and see how the cricket's getting along if you're sure you'll be all right." I picked up my cushion and went out into the sunshine.

I sat on a bench outside the pavilion and thought of the last match I had been to, of Thea so bright and happy in her cornflower blue dress and of Gordon Masefield, baiting Michael, arrogantly sure of himself. So much had happened since then, dreadful events that would leave their mark forever. The players cast long shadows in the late afternoon sun and a few yellow leaves, falling from the nearby trees, drifted across the pitch and I felt that sudden melancholy that comes with the realization that another summer is over and winter is not far away.

And I thought of Jackie, losing her baby in those miserable and sordid surroundings. I could only guess at what her feelings might have been. There may well have been some sense of relief, that now she wouldn't have to face her parents or struggle to make her way as a single parent in an unfriendly world. But there must also, surely, have been an agonizing sense of loss. To lose a baby, whatever the circumstances, is the most terrible thing that can happen to a woman, and she would have to face it alone, or, at the best, with a half-concerned, half-frightened casual acquaintance, who didn't really want to know.

"It was all for nothing." What did she mean by that? Did it mean that she had killed Gordon Masefield and now there was no reason for her to have done so? Perhaps. But, even as I watched with pleasure the white-clad figures moving across the green turf in their familiar ritual patterns, my heart ached for Jackie, whatever she might have done.

Chapter Thirteen

After that beautiful summer day the weather suddenly became autumnal and we had several days of driving rain and high winds. It was too unpleasant to go out unless one had to and I tried to occupy myself around the house, even to the extent of relining shelves in the pantry and turning out kitchen drawers.

"I wonder what on earth *this* is?" I enquired of Foss who, attracted by unusual activity in the kitchen, was standing on the work top hooking smaller objects out of the half-open drawer with his paws. He regarded the round metal object I was holding with scant attention and continued his own examination of the drawer.

"I think it must be some sort of patent of egg separator—no, it can't be. Wrong shape." I held it up to the light. "Perhaps it might be of some decorative value, on display somewhere. *Objet de fer enigmatique*. No, perhaps not." I threw the object into the bin and scrabbled about in the drawer again. This time I brought out two silver game skewers, one with a pheasant at its tip and the

other with a hare. I stood for a while looking
down at them in my hand. They were all that remained of a set of six that my mother had been
given as a wedding present and were very much a
part of my childhood—those far-off days when
even family meals were formal occasions. They
were very badly tarnished and I suddenly felt
guilty that they'd been thrust away in a drawer,
jumbled up with kitchen rubbish when a more
suitable, nobler repository should have been
found for them.

I got out the silver polish and a cloth and rubbed
away until, little by little, the tarnish was replaced
by a deep, satisfying shine. I thought I might give
them to Thea, together with my mother's Wedge-
wood dinner service that Michael and I never used
nowadays, even for dinner parties. But, I wondered, would Thea want to be burdened with these
relics of the past when she led such a busy life? I
was glad she'd gone back to work. She told me that
the first few days had been difficult. Not because of
the other people—they'd been kind and consider-
ate—but simply going up those stairs and facing
that closed door and remembering. Still, she was
back now and apparently absorbed in her work,
and life was going on, and if the question of Gordon Masefield's murder still hung over our lives
like some unpleasant miasma, well, we would
learn to live with it.

The following day the rain had stopped and,
eager to get out at last, I decided to go into Dunster
to buy a special kind of lardy cake that Michael is

very fond of. Since the tourist season was virtually over I was able to park relatively easily and stood for a moment looking from the old Yarn Market down the narrow, cobbled street to where the Castle, perched on a hill at the other end, seemed to crouch protectively over the village. I bought the cake and wandered aimlessly along, looking in the windows of the many gift shops, marveling at the way people will still buy souvenirs of an English village, even though those same objects are clearly labeled, "Made in Taiwan."

Having exhausted the delights of the main street, I turned into the narrow road that runs up behind the church and found myself outside a secondhand bookshop. The faded brown sign, above the door said BOOKS BOUGHT AND SOLD. The sign on the door said OPEN, though when I peered inside, the place seemed to be deserted. This, presumably, was Donald Masefield's bookshop. I stood for a while looking in the window. The books on display there were not so much arranged as dumped higgledy-piggledy in rows on dusty shelves. By twisting my head this way and that I was able to read a few of the titles. They were a varied lot from eighteenth-century sermons culled from some gentleman's library, to what appeared to be first editions of 1920s novels. It was the latter that lured me into the shop.

I don't know if it's true of everyone, but I find that the period I am most fascinated by is the one just before my own—that of my parents, in fact. I have always felt a particular affinity with the twenties and thirties, longed to have known the world before the war, yearned for the theater of Coward and Novello, and avidly devoured the more popular and thus more ephemeral novels of the period. I have a large collection of the works of Angela Thirkell, Stella Gibbons, and Rachel Ferguson and am forever haunting secondhand bookshops in an attempt (now increasingly forlorn) to find those volumes I still haven't got.

The door was quite stiff, as if no one had opened it for some time, and I had to give it quite a hard shove to get it open. It was dark inside, partly because of the nature of the shop, but also because of the vast quantity of books, not only on shelves, but also in unsteady piles on the floor, so that I had to pick my way among them with some care. There was a large square area immediately inside the door with a dark stairway to one side with a handwritten sign above it saying BIOGRAPHY, TRAVEL AND LOCAL INTEREST. As I moved further into the shop I came upon an alcove with a desk at which a young man was sitting with a large black dog at his feet. This, presumably, was Donald Masefield.

He was slightly built with brown hair already thinning and what seemed to be an anxious expression. As I approached he looked up from the book he was reading and the dog gave a bark and got to its feet.

"Quiet, Tess," he said, and, turning to me, "It's all right, she's quite harmless!"

I bent to stroke the dog. "I used to have a dog

called Tess, she was a spaniel. Is this one a cross-bred collie?"

"Yes, that's right."

"They're lovely. We had one when I was a child."

The dog, having decided that I was acceptable, settled down again at her master's feet and, laying her head on her paws, appeared to go to sleep.

The young man laid down his book. "Were you looking for anything special?" he asked.

"Well, yes. I collect the Victorian novels of Charlotte M. Yonge—not the historical ones. I've managed to find most of them but I'm still looking for *Three Brides* and *Beechcroft at Rockstone*. I don't suppose by any chance that you have either of those?"

He shook his head. "I'm afraid not. But I think I might be able to get you a copy of *Three Brides*. I seem to remember seeing it in a catalog the other day. It may be a bit pricey, though. Her books are quite collectable."

"Oh no," I said, "I don't mind the price—within reason, of course. That would be wonderful. It's quite difficult to get copies of the more obscure ones now. Odd, really, when you consider what a bestseller she was in her day and how many copies there must have been."

"A lot were pulped during the paper shortage in the war, of course, and, although there were some reprints of *The Heir of Redclyffe* in the thirties it's still mostly the Victorian editions that are still around."

"Oh, yes, I know, and the print is so *small*, I can hardly read them now by artificial light!"

He laughed, a pleasant and somehow unexpected sound. "Think what it must have been like by lamplight or candlelight," he said. He searched among the papers on the desk and produced an order book. "So shall I try and get that copy for you?"

"Yes, please." I gave him my name and address and added, "And if you ever find the other one, do please let me know."

"Of course."

"Splendid. Anyway, I'll just have a look around if I may?"

"Help yourself."

He got up and put on another light—a necessary gesture since the interior of the shop was very dark. The apparent chaos was misleading. As I had gathered from my brief conversation with him, Donald Masefield was thoroughly professional. The books were subdivided in a sort of simplified Dewey system and arranged alphabetically on the shelves. His prices, too, I noted, were just right—not so cheap that he wouldn't make a profit, but not so expensive that they would put off the casual buyer. Furthermore, the piles of books stacked about the place were all inexpensive, so that crouching on the floor and searching through them you were made to feel that you had found a bargain.

I did find several bargains, actually, and when I

went to pay for them I said, "Have you been here long? I haven't found the shop before."

"Not very long. We are a bit tucked away off the main street."

"Not much passing trade, then?"

"No. I do a lot of mail order, but the word is spreading and quite a few people have found their way here. Anyway, I don't really cater to the tourist trade."

"Well," I said, "I'll certainly tell *my* friends. There really aren't that many good secondhand book-shops around."

"That would be kind of you."

As I gave him the money for the books, I said, "You're Donald Masefield, aren't you?"

"Yes."

It was a flat statement of fact, but made slightly warily.

"I know your mother slightly and—and my son used to play cricket with your brother." I paused for a moment but there was no response, so I went on, "It was a dreadful thing, the way he died. I'm so sorry."

"Yes."

Again the flat statement and the wariness. I wondered how I could enlarge upon the subject of Gordon's death, but no suitable form of words came to me.

"Well . . ." I was just going to give it up as a bad job and take my leave, when the shop door opened and a young woman came in, awkwardly maneu-vering a pushchair across the threshold. Donald got to his feet and went over to help her and I recognized Wendy Masefield, Gordon's widow. The dog also got up and went over to the girl, wagging its tail as she bent forward and petted it. "Hello, Tess, good girl, then! Mandy, look, here's Tess come to say hello to you!" The little girl leaned out of her pushchair and stroked the smooth black head and the dog licked her hand.

I had withdrawn back into the shop, pretending to be examining some books on the shelves to my right so that Wendy didn't immediately see me.

"How's your mother?" Wendy asked Donald. "I thought I might call in this afternoon. Your father's in Taunton for the day, so . . ."

She left the sentence hanging in the air and he, seeming to understand the implication of her remark, said quickly, "That would be very good of you. She'd like that."

"She said the police had been round again. They wanted to check that you'd been together that afternoon." Donald made a quick gesture to indicate my presence and she broke off abruptly. I came forward and picked up my purchases from the desk.

"Thank you so much," I said, edging past Wendy and the pushchair, hoping she wouldn't recognize me. "I'll hope to hear from you, then."

"Hear. . . ?"

"About the Charlotte M. Yonge."

"Yes, yes, of course. Thank you. Good-bye."

I left the bookshop and went back down the hill, making for one of the many cafés that line the main street, so that I could sit down and consider what I had just seen.

"Would you like a fancy with your pot of tea?" the waitress asked. "Or we've got some lovely Devonshire splits. Clotted cream," she tempted.

"No, thank you," I said, my thoughts elsewhere. "Just the tea, please."

First of all, Donald Masefield wasn't the weak, ineffectual creature that I had imagined from Mrs. Dudley's scornful description—though, I suppose, she would despise anyone who kept a bookshop, not thinking anything to do with books a "proper job." His appearance, I felt, was deceptive. He seemed to be a competent businessman and the reticence I had noticed was certainly not due to shyness, but rather to a kind of watchful caution. No, there were definitely hidden depths there.

Then there was the appearance at the bookshop of Gordon Masefield's wife, Wendy. From her easy familiarity with the place, it would seem that she was a frequent visitor. Also, small girls don't usually pet large dogs with confidence unless they are very used to them. Wendy and her brother-in-law did seem to be on friendly terms. Were they, I wondered, more than friendly? According to Mrs. Dudley, it now seemed likely that Donald Masefield was the heir to a large fortune. That in itself would be a sufficient motive for murdering his brother, but if he was also in love with his brother's wife and had had to stand by and see her neglected and treated with contempt by her husband, the motive for killing him was even stronger.

Now that I knew there was a possibility of some unknown person slipping into the office unseen, it was reasonable to wonder if Donald might just be that person. In the brief remark she had made before Donald had silenced her, Wendy had said that Donald and his mother had each given the other an alibi. But it was not impossible that Harriet Masefield would have protected what I was sure was her favorite son, even in such circumstances. I poured myself a second cup of tea and considered the matter. From what Wendy had said in the shop, she seemed to be on good terms with Harriet Masefield, even though she only visited her when she knew that Roy would be away from home. And Donald's voice, when he spoke of his mother, had been somehow protective. I had felt a kind of intimacy between the three of them. In fact the few sentences that I overheard had told me quite a lot about those particular members of the Masefield family.

Of course, now I came to think of it, Wendy herself had been in the office the day of Gordon's murder. She hadn't gone upstairs but had only left the files she'd brought with Sally. Or, at least, so we thought. But Wendy might very well have left by the front door but then returned and come in the back way while Carol and Jackie were otherwise occupied. Her motive was much stronger now. If she wasn't just the wronged, neglected wife, but if she and Donald were in love (and I was sure that Gordon would never have given her up willingly to his despised younger brother) then, with no prospect of divorce, she might very well have had a powerful reason for wanting Gordon out of the way.

I wished I'd had the chance to observe her more closely. I only met her a couple of times before she was married, when she used to come to watch Gordon play cricket. She had seemed a shy, mousy sort of girl, who barely responded to conversation and didn't join in the social side of the cricket club. I'd asked her once if she'd like to help with the teas, but she'd murmured something about not having the time. But since I had been wrong about Donald, I began to wonder if I'd really got the measure of Wendy. After all, there must have been something about her that had attracted Gordon in the first place. She was pretty, but not spectacularly so, even then, before marriage to Gordon and having the baby had taken their toll. Perhaps she wasn't the little miss mouse she appeared, but altogether more clever, or, at least, more devious. Then there were her brothers—she must surely have had a fair amount of character to hold her own among three brothers! I would have to try and find someone who knew her better.

There were so many pieces that somehow might be fitted together, but I couldn't for the moment think how. My musings were interrupted by a party of pensioners urgently seeking cream teas, so I picked up my handbag and parcels and went out into the street. The rain had started again and I paused for a moment to find the scarf in my coat pocket to put over my head. The coach was parked outside, from which more pensioners were disembarking, and I heard one elderly lady say to another, "And he *wasn't* an accountant at all, just in the office. He'd been living a lie! Beryl *was* upset!"

Pondering this fascinating snippet I made my way cautiously over the wet cobbles on my way back to the car. Were Donald and Wendy what they seemed? For that matter, were any of us what we seemed to the outside world? Perhaps we were all, in one way or another, living a lie.

Chapter Fourteen

"You want to learn Italian?" I said to Rosemary. "Why?"

"Well," she replied, "I saw this television program about aging and I suddenly thought about all those brain cells dying off by the minute! So I thought I'd better do *something* while I still could."

"Oh, really!"

"No, honestly, I do feel I'm stagnating. It's all right for you, you've got your writing and reviewing and things, but I don't seem to have used my *mind* for thirty years! Anyway, this brochure thing about adult education evening classes popped through the letter box and I thought, why not?"

"But why Italian?"

"You know I've always wanted to go to Venice and I thought it would be nice to understand a bit of what they were saying."

"You've never got Jack to agree to go abroad?" I asked incredulously.

"Oh no, *he* won't go." She hesitated. "I thought you and I might. Next spring, perhaps. Well, Michael will be married then and I thought you might feel like a little trip . . ."

"Oh." I was a little taken aback at the idea.

"It would be fun."

"Yes," I said. "Yes, it would be. What a brilliant idea! I'd love to go."

"Oh, good. Then perhaps you'd come to the evening classes, too. I wasn't frightfully keen on going on my own."

"Was Venice a cunning ruse?"

"No, of course not! But do come to the classes. It might be a laugh."

"I must admit my Italian is minimal and I'd quite like to learn something new. All right, I'll do it. When's the first class?"

"In about a fortnight. Actually," she said, scrabbling in her bag, "I've got a spare enrollment form for you. I just brought it on the off chance."

When Rosemary had gone, I thought how lucky I was to have such a good friend. I knew perfectly well that the whole Venice thing was really to cheer me up because she knew that I'd be feeling miserable on my own after Michael had left home. That was something I was trying not to think about. It's been wonderful to have had him around for so long, and I'm really delighted that he's going to marry Thea—the perfect choice as far as I'm concerned—but I know it's going to be pretty desolate being on my own. I know I'll miss, too, the feeling of being needed—taken for granted sometimes, perhaps, but knowing that I'm essential to someone else's well-being.

A loud, peremptory cry interrupted my melancholy thoughts. Foss had come in through an open window and was urgently demanding his lunch and, as I began to get it, Tris, woken instantly from sleep by the infinitesimal sound of a can opener in operation, came scurrying into the kitchen also in search of food.

"Oh well," I said aloud as I put down the two bowls (a suitable distance apart), "I see I'm still needed for *something!*"

Tris looked up enquiringly at the sound of my voice, but Foss went on imperturbably eating. I laughed and got out the things for making a casserole for supper. Browning the meat, chopping carrots and celery, and crushing garlic were very soothing and if I had tears in my eyes it was not because of dismal thoughts and fears for the future, but simply because I was peeling onions.

A couple of days later I was standing at a checkout in the supermarket, wondering why I always chose the one where the till-roll had to be replaced by an inexperienced operative, who had to call the supervisor, who had, apparently, to take the whole thing to pieces to make it work, when a voice behind me said, "Hello, Sheila. Thinking deep thoughts?"

It was Roger.

"Good heavens," I said, "what are you doing here?"

"I'm on domestic duty. Jilly's housebound at the moment—Delia's got chicken pox."

"Oh, I *am* sorry. How is she?"

"The spots have come out, thank goodness, but she's very itchy, poor child, and it's a full-time job to keep her from scratching. We're hoping that Alex will get it too so that we can get it all over at once!"

"Poor Jilly must be exhausted, though I expect Rosemary is rallying round."

"She wanted to, but we wouldn't let her because of shingles. You know how you can get them from the chicken pox virus."

The moving belt with my groceries gave a lurch and moved forward and I had to start packing them into my shopping bag. When I had finished I turned to Roger and said, "Can you spare ten minutes? I'd like to ask you about something."

He looked at his watch. "Sure. I haven't got to collect Alex from play group until twelve thirty. Let's go and have a coffee."

When we were sitting in a relatively quiet corner of the Buttery I said, "I saw Donald Masefield the other day. I went into his shop."

Roger looked at me quizzically. "To buy a book, or to look him over?"

"A bit of both, I suppose."

"And?"

"For a start, he wasn't a bit like I expected—much more self-possessed and, I'd think, quite shrewd. What did you think of him?"

"Me?"

"I imagine you had to interview him. You've always said that money is often the main motive for murder, and Donald will be his father's heir now."

"Well, I don't know. There is Gordon Masefield's wife and daughter . . ."

"Not to be considered," I said, "at least according to your mother-in-law. Because they're females."

Roger laughed. "That has the authentic Dudley ring," he said.

"Actually, I think she might be right in this case. From what I've heard about Roy Masefield, he's likely to think that a son, however unsatisfactory in his terms, is better than any female. And, certainly, Wendy doesn't have the most forceful personality. So what about Donald?"

"You're right, there's certainly more to him than meets the eye. He was—how shall I put it?—cautious is perhaps the word. Didn't say a thing more than was necessary to answer any question."

"That's the impression I got. Where was he when Gordon was murdered?"

"In his shop."

"It's not exactly buzzing with customers. Did he have any witnesses?"

"His mother."

"Ah."

"He said she'd been there that afternoon to help him pack up some books for a large order he had."

"I think he does do quite a lot of mail orders. But no one else saw him there?"

"Apparently not. As you say, he doesn't seem to have many customers."

"So there's no way you can be sure he really was there? I mean, his mother would obviously cover for him."

"Even if he'd been killing his own brother, her other son?"

"Well, yes, I think so. If it really came down to it."

"Good heavens, it sounds like something out of Greek tragedy! But, of course, he couldn't have done it because someone would have seen him at the Barber and Freeman office."

"Ah, well, actually, there's something you really ought to know."

And I told him about Jackie and the baby.

"Poor Jackie was feeling very queasy all that day and Carol was with her in the ladies' loo a lot of the time. A whole *herd* of murderers could have come in the back way and they wouldn't have seen them."

"Good God! Why did no one tell me this before?"

"No one knew," I said placatingly, "except Carol, and she didn't feel she could betray Jackie's secret."

"And how did you find out? No, don't tell me, it's probably better that I don't know!"

"I haven't known for long," I said, slightly mendaciously. "But it does alter things, doesn't it?"

"It certainly puts Donald Masefield high up on the list of suspects and opens up the door to a lot of other possibilities . . ." He broke off. "Oh Lord, I forgot to get the Calpol for Delia. I must dash to the chemist before I collect Alex. Look, we must have another talk about this." He got to his feet and picked up his supermarket bags. "I'll give you a ring."

"Give my love to Jilly," I said, "and I do hope Delia is better soon."

It felt very strange to be back in a classroom again.

"It's just as well children don't sit at desks any more," I said to Rosemary as we sat uneasily at small tables. "We'd never have fitted into those."

I looked around at our fellow students who were gradually filing into the room. There were two quiet young men, four girls in their twenties, and two retired couples. I wondered what reasons they all had for being there—no doubt it would become apparent as the classes progressed. Just before the class was due to begin one more person came in. She entered hesitantly, as if she wasn't sure she was in the right place. It was Harriet Masefield. I nudged Rosemary, who hadn't noticed her, and she called out, "Harriet! Fancy seeing you here! Come and sit with us."

Harriet gave us both a nervous smile and sat down, rather reluctantly I thought, at our table.

"How nice to see you," Rosemary said in the bracing tone she keeps for jollying along unenthusiastic helpers at jumble sales. "Have you come to extend your horizons like us?"

Harriet gave her the same nervous smile. "I suppose you could say that," she said.

She didn't seem anxious to elaborate on this and seemed relieved when the door opened and the class fell silent.

The smell of chalk and dust, with just a hint of disinfectant, is as powerfully evocative as Proust's madeleine so I was in a rather subdued mood, and, when our Italian teacher came in, I had to resist a strong impulse to rise to my feet and answer, "Present," as we used to do to Miss Alcock in primary school when the class register was taken.

Sharon Rossiter, our teacher, is a nice girl in her middle thirties. She teaches modern languages at the local comprehensive school and is very brisk and efficient.

"We'll start off with a few Italian phrases," she said, "just to give you a taste of the language before we get down to the nitty-gritty of the grammar."

She distributed lists of words and phrases, telling us to try them out on each other and a confused babble of English and Italian broke out.

"Here's a good one for me," Rosemary said. "*Ne ha uno piu grande?* That means, have you anything bigger?"

I laughed. "I like these: *Mi dia una pomata control punture d'insetti*—that's I want something for insect bites. Then there's, *Penso che sia avvelenato*—I think it's poisoned. Then *Chiami subito un'ambulanza!*—call an ambulance quickly!"

"Goodness," Rosemary exclaimed. "Perhaps we'd better avoid Venice after all! I'm sure it's seething with mosquitoes—all that water!"

I turned to Harriet. "How about you? Have you found any good ones?"

She gave a tight little smile and said, "Not really."

"A lavatory is WC," Rosemary said. "Perhaps that's really all we need to know!"

After a few minutes Sharon Rossiter called us to order and began the lesson proper. I tried very hard to concentrate as she gave us the basic elements of the grammar, but I found my mind wandering to the problem of Harriet Masefield and what she was doing here. As far as I could see, she didn't seem particularly enthusiastic. Not that she looked like the sort of person who would be enthusiastic about anything. A strange lot, these Masefields!

"'A' 'an' or 'one' is translated 'un' before a masculine noun," Sharon was saying, "and 'una' before a feminine noun. 'Uno' is used instead of 'un' before an s impure (when s is followed by a consonant) and before z. 'Un' is substituted for 'una' before a vowel . . ."

"*What's* an s impure?" Rosemary whispered. "It sounds improper!"

"I haven't the faintest," I whispered back. And then, because whispering in class had always been one of the things that had got us into trouble when we were at school, we both had to stifle giggles and Sharon looked at us disapprovingly, which almost set us off again.

When the lesson was over a small group gathered around Sharon, presumably seeking further enlightenment, but Rosemary and I began to gather up our workbooks and the vocabulary lists we'd been given.

"Well," Rosemary said doubtfully, "I don't know if I'm going to be able to get to grips with all this!"

"Of course you will," I said reassuringly.

She shook her head. "I think my brain has atrophied. All that grammar sounds so complicated!"

"I agree it does seem a bit formidable, but I'm sure it's only because we're out of practice." I turned to Harriet. "What do you think?"

She looked flustered, as if she wasn't used to having her opinion sought. "I don't know. It did seem quite difficult . . ."

"Come on, both of you," I said, "we can't give up after the first lesson!"

"And all this *homework*," Rosemary said in disgust. "I thought I'd put that behind me years ago!"

"Nonsense," I said firmly, "it will do you good!"

"What I really need for all this lot," Rosemary said, struggling to put the assortment of papers into a plastic carrier bag, "is a *satchel*!"

"I don't think children have satchels any more," I said, "only those sort of knapsack things they all seem to carry with Barbie pictures or Star Trek stickers on them."

"Oh, whatever!" Rosemary said, then turning to Harriet she said, "We're going to get a coffee. Do come with us?"

Harriet hesitated. "It's very kind of you, but Donald will be waiting to drive me back."

"Oh, I met your son the other day," I said. "I went into his shop—he's getting a book for me."

She seemed pleased and murmured something that I didn't catch.

"I was very sorry to hear about Gordon," Rosemary said.

Harriet was silent for a moment and I wondered if Rosemary's remark had upset her. But her expression didn't change and she merely said, "It was very sad." She picked up her books and said, "I must go now."

"See you next week," I said.

"Yes, possibly—yes, I expect so."

"What a peculiar thing to say!" Rosemary exclaimed. " 'Very sad.' "

"It was an odd thing to say," I agreed, "when your son's been murdered."

"Well, she is odd." Rosemary picked up her handbag. "The hell with coffee, I could do with a drink after all those wretched nouns and things. I just hope Venice is going to be worth all this effort!"

A few days later I had a neat, handwritten card from Donald Masefield to say that he'd got hold of a copy of *Three Brides*, so that afternoon I went into Dunster to collect it.

The shop was, as I had expected, empty of customers. Donald Masefield was not sitting at his desk, but engaged in sorting through a box of books by the stairs. He looked up as I entered.

"Residue of a house sale," he said. "Sometimes there's something interesting, but mostly it's junk."

"Is that lot junk?" I asked.

"No, actually, there's some good military history stuff here. That always sells well."

I moved across to him and began turning over some of the books.

"Goodness, it's sad," I said. "Books are so *personal*. I can't bear to think of any of my books being got rid of when I'm gone but, of course, they'll have to be. My son will keep some, but an awful lot of them won't mean anything to anyone but me."

He gave me a brief smile. "Yes, it sometimes gets to me, especially if it's obviously a lifetime's collection, lovingly put together over the years. I always try to keep collections together, but it's not always possible."

He got up from the floor where he had been kneeling and went over to the desk.

"Here's the Charlotte M. Yonge *Three Brides*," he said. "It's rather an interesting copy, actually."

"Oh, really?"

"Yes. It's the 1883 edition and the illustrations are by Adrian Stokes."

"That sounds very good."

"What makes it particularly interesting is the fact that there is an autographed letter written by Adrian Stokes pasted in it."

He handed the book to me and I examined it with interest.

"Oh, it's the brown and gold binding," I said, "not the usual blue one. That's nice. And I think the print is ever so slightly bigger than the other editions, which is just as well!" I opened the book and looked at the letter. "Adrian Stokes appears to be living in St. Ives at the time. I wonder if it was a center for artists in those days as it is now? He says he's just off to Paris and can't dine with this Mr. Spielman and encloses a cheque for one guinea for the Artists' General Benevolent Fund. That was quite a lot of money. He must have been doing well!"

"I imagine book illustration in the late nineteenth century was a growth industry," Donald Masefield said.

"Goodness, yes. And they all looked very much the same. Those strong-jawed ladies and the wonderful domestic detail, the delicate lines of the drawing and all that cross-hatching, if that's what it's called."

"They are very pleasant," he agreed, "if you have a taste for that particular period."

"Oh, I love Victorian novels. That feeling of safety—even though such melodramatic things happen—that solid ground! I suppose, in the case of Charlotte M. Yonge, it's the strong religious element, the complete certainty of faith. Though some people are allowed to have doubts, they are always resolved in the end."

"I know what you mean, but I find her world too constricted, too stifling. When it comes to Victorian religion I prefer a lighter touch. I go for Trollope myself."

"Yes, I can see that. I love Trollope, but he doesn't

give me the sort of *virtuous* feeling I get after reading Charlotte M. Yonge."

He laughed. "Ah, that's a different thing entirely."

I put the book down on the desk. "Now then," I said, "what do I owe you?"

He named a very modest sum.

"Are you sure?" I asked. "That sounds more than reasonable."

"Ah well, let's call it a sprat to catch a mackerel. Now you will come back, I hope, and buy a lot of other books."

"I'll certainly do that."

"Actually, I got it very reasonably myself. And I do have hopes of getting a copy of *Beechcroft at Rockstone* for you from the same source."

"That would be marvelous. I've been looking for it for ages."

"I suppose, to be strictly honest," he said, "I ought to tell you that you could probably have found both of them on the Internet."

"Oh, I could never do that," I exclaimed. "The horror of computers! All that sort of thing is quite beyond me."

"It's the way of the future, I'm afraid."

"Not for me," I said firmly. "Any more than I can measure in centimeters or weigh in kilos, and every so often I change prices back into old money and am appalled to find that a small brown loaf costs over ten shillings."

"One must never look back."

"When you're my age it's fatally easy! Still, I do

like to try something new. Which reminds me, I saw your mother at our Italian class this week, so she must feel the same way."

"It was my idea that she should go," he said. "I thought it might do her good—cheer her up."

"Yes, of course," I said. "She must have been dreadfully upset, about your brother, I mean."

"It's all been a bit of a strain," he said. "My father's still convinced it was that girl—the one who was arrested—who killed him."

"Thea Wyatt," I said, "the girl who was arrested, is engaged to my son, Michael."

He looked confused. "I'm so sorry. I didn't believe, myself—I mean, the police released her—I'm sure she's innocent . . . Do forgive me."

"You weren't to know, they haven't officially announced their engagement. But she is innocent. They have proved that. With the help of a computer, actually, so they do have their uses."

"With the help of a computer?" He looked at me enquiringly.

"Oh, something to do with times, I don't understand the details. It was enough for me that it established Thea's innocence. It was a terrible time for us all when she was arrested and detained in prison."

"It must have been."

"Still," I said, "so much worse for your mother to lose a son. I didn't know him well, of course, I just saw him at cricket matches. Were you very close?"

He shook his head. "Not really. Actually, not at all. We were too different, even as children. And then, in recent years . . ." He broke off, as if remembering that he was talking to a stranger. "No, we didn't really get on."

There was a rustling sound and the black dog came in from the back of the shop. She gave Donald Masefield an enquiring look and then settled down at his feet. I bent to stroke her.

"Hello, Tess," I said. "Aren't you beautiful!"

She raised her head and licked my hand.

"She's very friendly," I said, "and very sweet."

"She's hoping for a walk. Sometimes, when things are quiet, I take her down onto Dunster beach. There's no garden to speak of here."

"Oh, do you live over the shop?"

"Yes, it's handy. There's quite a large flat upstairs." He bent down and patted the dog. "No walks today, old girl. Too much to do." He looked up. "My mother takes her sometimes or—or a friend." He began to put the books on his desk into a pile. "I'll let you know if I can get that other Charlotte M. Yonge."

"That will be lovely," I said. "But I expect I'll be dropping in next time I'm this way."

As I left the shop and turned down the hill to where I'd left the car, I wondered if the "friend" who took Tess for a walk was Wendy, and what, exactly, their relationship might be.

Chapter Fifteen

I hate cleaning the oven. Well, I don't know anyone who likes it, really. My main oven is said to be self-cleaning but I hardly ever use it because I'm beginning to find bending down with a large, hot casserole dish in my oven-gloved hands is becoming quite dangerous, so I put everything into the smaller oven, which is also a grill and therefore seems to need cleaning more often. I got out the oven cleaner with the terrifying information about its caustic qualities, spread newspaper over the floor in case of drips, and put on my plastic gloves. I gave a couple of tentative squirts only to find that the aerosol can was empty. Having psyched myself up to the task, I was determined to carry it through.

"Right then," I said to Tris, who had just pushed his way into the kitchen. "I'll have to go out to get some more." At the word "out" Tris gave an excited bark. "No," I said, "not that sort of out. Oh dear, all right, you can come, too."

I had intended to go straight back home when I'd bought the oven cleaner, but Tris's pleading glances and eager whining made that quite impossible so I found myself parking by the sea wall and following him down the steps onto the beach. There was another dog walker in the far distance but the only other people on the beach were a woman with two small children. As I got nearer I saw that it was Jilly with Delia and Alex. I waved and went to greet them, Tris rushing on ahead of me, barking madly.

"Hello!" I called out. "Fancy seeing you here! Tris, stop that—you'll frighten Delia."

Delia looked up from her intent perusal of the beach. "*I'm* not frightened," she said. "I'm a fairy princess and I'm looking for my magic seashell. *He*"—she indicated her brother, who was poking about with a stick in a rock pool—"might be frightened because he's only little."

By then Tris had rushed past the children and was pursuing a seagull.

"I thought I'd bring them for a runabout on the beach after school, just to wear them out," Jilly said. "In the vain hope of getting them to bed at a reasonable hour. Since Delia's been home with chicken pox—at least, now she's more or less better—she seems to stay up till all hours."

"She looks fine now," I said.

"Oh, she is—back at school, thank goodness."

"And how about Alex? Did he get it, too?"

"No such luck. He'll probably come down with it just when we're due to go on holiday or something!"

"Talking of holidays, I gather you had a wonderful time in America."

"Oh, it was fabulous—Americans are so kind! But I was so sorry to hear about all that business while we were away. It must have been ghastly for you all. How is Thea now?"

"Oh, all right, I think. Just about. It's going to take her quite a while to get over it."

"I was so pleased to hear about her and Michael. We'd love them to come to dinner sometime soon."

"I'm sure they'd love to—but not quite yet. I think Thea might find it a bit difficult, with Roger, until all this is cleared up."

"Yes, of course, not the most tactful idea of mine!" She broke off and called to Delia, "Don't let Alex throw that seaweed about, he'll get covered in sand!"

Delia, who had found a large mussel shell, waved it at her brother and said in a menacing tone, "This is my fairy shell and if you aren't good I'll magic you into a frog!"

"Frog! Frog!" Alex shouted and, shrieking with laughter, began hopping about in what he imagined to be a froglike way.

Jilly turned back to me. "Mind you, from what I've heard, Gordon Masefield was a pretty loathsome sort of person. What that poor girl Wendy had to put up with! Still, his poor mother was dreadfully upset. Well, she would be, of course."

"It's a terrible thing to lose a child, however unsatisfactory," I said.

We both turned to look at Delia and Alex, now

racing round in circles, delighting in making fresh footsteps in the sea-washed sand.

"Yes," Jilly said, "it must be. Poor Harriet Masefield. Chloe—that's the girl who does my hair—was full of the murder. Her mother used to do cleaning for the Masefields, so she knew all about the family. She was the one who told me about Harriet."

"What was that?"

"Well, apparently, on the afternoon it happened Chloe was fetching her little boy from school (she only works mornings now) and they always walk home through that little park, you know the one, at the far end of the town. They always go that way because Gavin—that's her little boy—likes to look at the ducks on the pond. Anyway, as they got to the pond they saw Harriet Masefield sitting on the bench there. She had a child in a pushchair, so I suppose it was Wendy's little girl. Chloe was just going up to speak to her when she saw that Harriet was crying—I mean, really *crying*, real sobs. So she turned back and went the long way round. I suppose Harriet had just heard about Gordon. Chloe said she felt awful leaving her like that, but she really didn't think she could intrude. She'd no idea then what it was all about. Of course, when the word got around about the murder, she realized why Harriet was in that state, poor soul."

"What time was this?" I asked.

"I don't know, really. I suppose Chloe fetched Gavin from school at three o'clock so it would be about three thirty to a quarter to four."

"But the murder wasn't discovered until four o'-clock," I said, "so it can't have been that. I wonder what it was, why she was so unhappy?"

"I should think being married to Roy Masefield would be enough to make anyone unhappy," Jilly said.

"Mummy, Mummy!" Delia called. "Alex has got all wet!"

We went over to where the children were playing. Alex was standing knee-deep in a rockpool, flapping his hands about in the water. He gave us a beaming smile. "Fish," he said. "Fish in water!"

"Oh, Alex!" Jilly said, hauling him out. "You're absolutely *soaking*! Look at your shoes and socks! Delia, why didn't you stop him?"

"I said you'd be cross," Delia said smugly. "I said Mummy *will* be cross. She'll magic you into a spider!"

"Oh, Lord!" Jilly said helplessly. "He's dripping! He'll make a dreadful mess of the car! I wouldn't mind, but mine's in for a service and I had to borrow Roger's and you know what men are like about their precious cars!"

"I've got an old dog-walking anorak in the back of my car," I said. "You could wrap Alex up in that."

"Bless you, Sheila, that would be marvelous. Come on, you two, before anyone gets a chill standing about here."

*   *   *

"Wasn't that odd?" I said to Michael. "Sitting there crying on that very afternoon, just about the time Gordon was killed. Almost as if she knew."

"Perhaps she did," Michael said.

"What do you mean?"

"Well, if she was sitting in this park she certainly wasn't with Donald in the shop, like she said she was. So perhaps Donald was out killing his brother and she knew what he was going to do."

"Oh no," I exclaimed, "she couldn't!"

"Well, perhaps she didn't actually *know* what was happening, but she might have suspected."

"That's too horrible. It's—it's like some sort of Jacobean tragedy!"

"Well, in deference to your sensibilities, we'll say she didn't know what Donald was up to, but the fact remains that if they weren't together then neither of them has an alibi."

"No," I said, "that's not true. It's only Donald who hasn't got one. She was seen by an independent witness miles away from Gordon's office at just about the time of the murder. So she does have an alibi. Only it's not the one she gave to the police."

"So why should she have pretended to be with Donald that afternoon?"

"Presumably because he was up to something illegal."

"Like murdering his brother. *Quod erat demonstrandum.*"

"Oh dear, it does sound suspicious."

"Are you going to tell Roger what you've just discovered?"

"I suppose I ought to . . ."

"But?"

"Well, Harriet Masefield is such a pathetic creature . . ."

"You don't want her bullied by a big, ferocious policeman?"

"No, Roger's not like that and you know it! No, I just wondered if, before I did that, I could somehow find out what was really going on."

It was in pursuit of this aim that I drove over to Dunster the next afternoon. As I walked up the hill I turned over in my mind what I could possibly ask Donald Masefield that might throw light on the mystery without alerting him to my suspicions. I couldn't think of anything at all and I was in half a mind to turn round and go back home when I reached the shop. As it turned out I needn't have worried because the place was shut, with a CLOSED notice on the door. I tried the handle but it was locked. I stepped back on the pavement and looked up at the first-story windows and I thought I saw a curtain twitch, but as I kept looking there was no sign of life and I thought I must have imagined it.

Two doors along there was a newsagent and I went in. There was no one else in the shop and, picking up a magazine from the stand, I went over to the counter.

"You don't happen to know if the bookshop's closed all day?" I asked, proffering a coin for the magazine.

The middle-aged man behind the counter shook his head.

"Couldn't say," he said. "He's a law unto himself is that one."

"Really?"

"Sometime he's shut, sometime's he's open—no rhyme or reason to it."

"How strange."

"Can't think how he makes any sort of living, going on the way he does."

"It does seem odd."

"Downright stupid, if you ask me. Times are difficult enough as it is, what with the Council putting up the rates—council tax, whatever they call them now—absolutely criminal! How we're expected to make a living . . ." He went to the till and handed over my change. "No, you need to work every hour God sends just to keep going nowadays. Take me. Open seven days a week, all hours, and the paper-round. I usually have to deliver them myself when that useless boy doesn't show up!"

"What's he like?"

"Like? Who?"

"The person who has the bookshop."

"Oh, him. Don't know, really. Keeps to himself. Just about passes the time of day and that's it. Don't know what a real day's work is, people like that. I've been in the trade thirty years now, took over from my uncle . . ."

He seemed inclined to continue in this vein so I picked up the magazine from the counter and, making what I hoped were sympathetic noises, backed out of the shop.

When I returned to the car I tossed the magazine onto the seat beside me. Looking down I saw that the lead story, featured on the cover, was Twenty Ways to Tell If Your Man Is Cheating on You. Poor little Wendy Masefield, I thought, didn't need a magazine article to find out about Gordon, there were plenty of people in Taviscombe only too ready to tell her that.

"So," I reported back to Michael that evening, "if the hours of the bookshop are that erratic and Harriet *wasn't* there, then Donald could perfectly well have murdered his brother. Let's face it, he had the best motive. Unless Roy Masefield alters his will, he'll inherit a lot of money."

"Yes, but his father's still reasonably young and in perfectly good health, as far as any of us know, so why go and kill Gordon now?"

"All right. Perhaps that wasn't the primary motive. How about Wendy?"

"What do you mean, 'How about Wendy?'"

"Well, it's perfectly obvious that Donald likes her, probably more than likes. Perhaps he couldn't stand it any more, to see her being treated like that by Gordon. Perhaps he wants to marry her himself."

"You don't have to murder someone nowadays if you want to marry their wife. There's such a thing as divorce. Believe me, I'm a lawyer!"

"I don't know. Can you imagine that Gordon would just sit back and let Wendy divorce him so that she could marry his younger brother, who he despised? Not very likely, is it? Gordon would have made things impossibly unpleasant. He'd have had Roy on his side for a start, so Harriet would have been made miserable, too. No, I don't think divorce was an option. I still think it was a good reason for Donald to murder Gordon."

"You may be right. So you think Donald could have slipped in when no one was looking—no, hang on. I don't see how he could have planned it in advance. For a start, how would he have known there'd be no one in that back office, so that he could get in there without being seen?"

I thought for a moment, then I said triumphantly, "Wendy! She was there earlier. She might have seen that Carol and Jackie weren't around when she was there, or, more likely, Carol may have told her that Jackie was feeling ill, though obviously she wouldn't have said why!"

"Ye-es, I suppose it's possible. So Wendy went back and told Donald, who promptly shut the shop and went and murdered Gordon."

"Well, why not?"

"It's possible, I suppose."

"You don't sound convinced. You must admit that Donald is a more likely murderer than Wendy!"

"Yes, I grant you that. It's just that it all sounds a bit chancy."

"Nonsense," I said robustly. "I think it's a perfectly good theory. Anyway, it's the best we've got so far."

"Even if it is right, I don't see how you're going to prove it. Or are you going to tell Roger and let him work out the finer details?"

"Oh dear, yes," I said guiltily. "I suppose I really ought to let him know about Harriet's alibi being useless."

"Well, then . . ."

"I'll just give it another day or so. Perhaps something might turn up."

"Such as?"

"I don't know—don't hassle me! I just want to give it a bit longer, that's all."

"It's up to you. Anyway, I must be off. I'm picking up Thea at six thirty. We thought we'd drive over to Lynmouth and have dinner at the Sun."

"That's nice, it'll cheer her up. I thought she was a bit piano when I saw her on Saturday."

"She does her best, poor love, but she won't be her old self until this wretched business is over."

"Then," I said firmly, "we must get a move on and get it sorted. I'm sure we're on the right track. All it needs is a little application!"

Chapter Sixteen

"Oh, look, Hugh Barber's back!"

We were walking down Park Street when Rosemary pointed up at the second floor of the Barber and Freeman offices, where Hugh could be seen standing in the large bay window speaking into a small dictaphone.

"Oh yes, so he is," I said. "I wonder how they got on on their cruise and how Lois is."

"Well, if Hugh's back at work she can't be too bad."

We turned into the Buttery and found a table at the back away from the door.

"I'll get the coffees," I said. "Do you want a Danish?"

"I ought not to . . . What are you having?"

"I'm going to have one."

"Oh, all right, I will, too."

"If you were as ill as Lois," Rosemary said when we were settled, "would *you* want to go traipsing round the world?"

"No way," I said firmly. "I mean, I wouldn't want to go on a cruise even if I was really well—

shut up with probably uncongenial people all that time and no way to escape—but, no, I think I'd want to stick in my own familiar surroundings."

"Goodness, yes," Rosemary said. "The importance of one's own *bed*! Lois always was one for traveling, though. I suppose if you're like that anyway, you want to go on as you've always done. Mind you, she's got guts, you must admit!"

"Oh yes. She's always been very resolute about getting what she wanted and doing what she wanted to do. I suppose that sort of attitude, even if it made life difficult for other people when she was well, is invaluable in her present situation."

"Yes, poor old Hugh. He has been more or less dragged along behind her all these years. But he adores her, so I suppose that's all right."

"I can't imagine how he'll cope when she's gone," I said. "No children, practically no family of any kind—he'll be desolated."

"I must say I hope Jack goes before me," Rosemary said, stirring her coffee meditatively. "He would be absolutely useless on his own and I don't see him marrying again. I suppose women cope better in these circumstances." She looked up at me. "You did."

"Well, I had to, because of Michael, if for nothing else."

"That's what I mean. We can usually find something or someone who still needs us. I remember when Harry died, Ursula said she didn't think she'd have wanted to go on, but she had to get out of bed in the mornings to see to the dogs!"

"Oh well, the animals . . . Do you know, I believe Foss is in his second kittenhood. He's roaring around the place wanting to *play* all the time. I have to keep twiddling a piece of string for him to leap out at. And he's taken to carrying it around in his mouth and dropping it at my feet and demanding that I play with him. I suppose he's seen Tris work that trick with a ball."

"How sweet!"

"It's very tiring."

I had the opportunity of asking Hugh about Lois the very next day when he was parked behind me in the filling station. He got out of his car and came over to talk to me.

"Sheila, how are you all?"

"Oh, hello, Hugh. We're fine. At least Michael and I are . . ."

"I thought Thea seemed to have recovered very well from her dreadful ordeal. I was so glad to see her back at work."

"She's putting a brave face on it, but it will take some time before she's back to normal."

"No, I can understand that."

I removed the petrol nozzle from my car and hitched it back onto the pump.

"How's Lois? Did she enjoy the cruise?"

"I think so—no, I'm sure she did. It was all a bit exhausting for her, though, and she's not too well at the moment."

"I'm so sorry."

"I expect she'll perk up when she's had a few days' rest."

He seemed unwilling to elaborate and I didn't feel I could press him.

"I'm sure she will," I said. "Oh, goodness, there's quite a queue forming, I'd better get on."

While I was waiting to pay my bill inside, I looked through the window at Hugh and was struck by his tense expression and general air of unhappiness. I could only conclude that Lois was much worse than he would admit, perhaps even to himself.

I said as much to Thea when she came round to supper that evening.

"He does seem very preoccupied and worried," she said. "He's hardly done anything in the office since he got back, and, you can imagine, things have rather piled up since he's been away, though we have done our best to keep the backlog at bay."

"Is that what you do to a backlog?" Michael said. "I've often wondered."

"Idiot—you know what I mean. Jonah's been very overworked and I think I told you that Eileen Newton's done a lot of things that aren't strictly her job. She's very conscientious but awfully slow!"

"A good legal exec," Michael said judicially, "can frequently be a darned sight more useful than an indifferent assistant solicitor. I think you're jolly lucky to have a pearl like that. We'd be very happy to head-hunt her any day!"

"I don't think she'd come to you. I suspect she's got a bit of a crush on Hugh."

"He used to be immensely attractive when he was a young man," I said. "I suppose he still is in a way, but he's aged so much in the last year. Not surprising, I suppose."

"Your friend Roger Eliot came in to see him yesterday," Thea said.

"Really? What for, do you know?"

"Oh, just general checking up, I gather. I think he wanted to ask Hugh about a few things that have come to light since he's been away."

"He surely doesn't suspect Hugh!"

"No, nothing like that. He's got a perfectly good alibi. Actually Inspector Eliot's been in and out several times, confirming alibis and taking away papers—that sort of thing. I suppose the police have to give the impression that they're doing *something*."

There was a note of bitterness in her voice so I hastened to change the subject.

"So have you both decided yet which weekend you're going up to London to stay with Cousin Hilda?"

"We thought the weekend after next," Michael said. "If that suits her. I'll ring tomorrow and see."

"I must say," Thea said, "I'm absolutely terrified of meeting her. She sounds really formidable. And I gather that she adores Michael, so she's bound to think I'm not good enough for him!"

Michael and I exchanged glances and smiled.

"She *was* formidable," I said, "but then she got involved with this Siamese . . ."

"Siamese?" Thea looked puzzled. "Oh, you mean a Siamese *cat*!"

"That's right. She *dotes* on him. So all you have to do is make a fuss of Tolly and she's your friend for life."

Thea laughed. "I think I can manage that," she said. "Oh, did I tell you that Smoke has learned how to use the cat flap that Michael put in for me?"

"How splendid. I do wish I could have a cat flap here, but in an old house like this all the doors are too thick to cut holes in. So I just have to let Foss in and out, and very boring it is, too!"

I'd meant to have a word with Harriet Masefield after our next Italian class. After my failure to see Donald, I thought I might try and see what I could get out of her. But she didn't turn up, so I was frustrated again.

"What's happened to Harriet?" I asked Rosemary. "Did you hear anything?"

"Sharon said that she's not coming again. She's given up."

"Really?"

"Yes, apparently she said she found it too difficult. Isn't it feeble of her?"

"What a shame."

"Did you hear about Mrs. York?" Rosemary asked, lowering her voice and indicating the female half of one of the retired couples sitting in the front row.

"No. What?"

"She's been working away like mad—even had private lessons—and she's got on to the *subjunctive*!"

"Good heavens! Why?"

"Well," Rosemary's whisper was practically inaudible, "apparently she's got an Italian daughter-in-law whom she hates, and she's learning Italian so that she can tell her exactly what she thinks of her!"

"In the subjunctive?" I asked.

Sharon called the class to order then, but while she was telling us about pronunciation ("Remember that each letter in Italian is pronounced separately and distinctly, so double consonants must be pronounced twice: essa is ess-sah, say it after me . . .") I was wondering if Harriet had really found Italian too difficult or if she was simply avoiding people who might want to talk about Donald and Gordon and what had happened. And then, in contrast to Mrs. York, I thought about Harriet and her daughter-in-law.

"Mrs. Malory." Sharon's voice broke in on my thoughts. "Can you tell me the names of the days of the week?"

"Oh dear—*lunedì, martedì, mercoledì, giovedì*—um—sorry I've forgotten Friday . . ."

Mrs. York's hand waved impatiently. "*Venerdì, sabato, domenica*," she reeled off, giving me a scornful look.

"That's put you in *your* place," Rosemary said

sotto voce as I collected my thoughts and tried to concentrate on the rest of the lesson.

"It's a pity about Harriet giving up," I said to Rosemary as we were leaving the classroom after the lesson, "I'm sure she needs to be taken out of herself and given some sort of interest."

"I suppose so. But I don't know that learning a foreign language is going to change her personality, do you? I mean, she's always been a dim sort of person, a born doormat, and I don't think she's suddenly going to get a new and vibrant personality if she can say 'I want a shampoo and set' in Italian."

"No, but it would be something she'd done on her own. Actually, I'm surprised Roy Masefield allowed her to do anything as revolutionary as go to evening classes."

"Oh he's too busy with his new girlfriend, didn't I tell you?"

"No! Really? Who is it?"

"I don't know her name. Janis was in the middle of telling me about it all when she had to go and see about Anthea's rinse."

Janis is Rosemary's hairdresser and a very fruitful source of Taviscombe gossip.

"So what *did* she say?"

"Well, apparently Roy Masefield's been seen in a pub in Dulverton with this woman. Not particularly young, Janis said, but very smart—lots of makeup and masses of blond hair. I suppose she comes from round there. I can't imagine he'd be bothered about being seen with her in Taviscombe.

After all she isn't the first and I don't suppose she'll be the last. He's been unfaithful to Harriet from practically the first year they were married!"

"It's easy to see where Gordon got his roving eye from!"

"Yes, both thoroughly nasty pieces of work. And both their wives, Harriet and Wendy, are meek little creatures who daren't say boo to a goose."

"Poor Harriet. It's worse for her—to have had both a husband *and* a son like that. No wonder she clings to Donald."

"She adores Wendy's little girl," Rosemary said. "I see her almost every day in the town, with the little girl in a pushchair."

I did, in fact, see Harriet Masefield and the child the following day. They were in the little park, where Chloe had seen her on the day of Gordon's murder. This time she looked more cheerful and was patiently encouraging the little girl to throw bread to the ducks.

"Hello, Harriet," I said, "Isn't it a lovely day."

She turned round quickly and I was distressed to see how suddenly she changed from quiet happiness to a tense sort of anxiety.

"Oh hello Sheila," she said uncertainly.

I bent over the pushchair. "Hello Mandy," I said. "Are you helping Gran feed the ducks?"

Harriet gave me a wary smile.

"There's something about ducks, isn't there?" I said. "Something that children seem to respond to. I know Michael always preferred feeding the ducks to going onto the beach to feed the seagulls. I suppose seagulls can be quite menacing to a child."

This bland chat seemed to help Harriet relax and she even proferred a few mild remarks of her own, so that it seemed quite natural that I should sit down on the seat beside her.

We talked for a while about the weather and other innocuous topics while Harriet moved the pushchair gently backward and forward.

"She didn't sleep much last night," she said, "poor little mite. She's cutting a back tooth and it kept her awake, Wendy said, so I'll be glad if she can get a little nap."

"Michael was a dreadfully bad sleeper," I said. "For ages he'd only drop off in the car. I can remember Peter having to drive him around in the middle of the night for hours on end!"

"Mandy likes the pushchair," Harriet said, apparently further reassured by my domestic revelations. "I can usually get her off in that. Yes, look, she's fast asleep now."

We both looked down at the sleeping child and smiled at each other.

"We like coming here," Harriet said. "It's nice and quiet."

"You were here that day, weren't you?"

I felt mean confronting her like this after I had encouraged her to relax. I felt I was betraying her trust, but it seemed too good an opportunity to miss.

She looked at me with frightened eyes. "What day?" she asked, almost in a whisper.

"The day Gordon was killed. Someone saw you here that afternoon."

She shook her head blindly. "No, no!" she said. "They must have been mistaken!"

"No. There was no mistake. Chloe Middleton saw you here at about four o'clock—the time you told the police that you were with Donald at the shop."

She didn't question how I knew these things but just stared at me, still shaking her head in a denial she obviously knew was useless.

"Harriet," I said gently, "if you weren't with Donald, where was he?"

Her eyes widened and she seemed suddenly to understand what I was suggesting.

"Oh, no!" she cried. "You can't think *he* killed Gordon!"

"But he had cause, didn't he?"

"No, that's not true. He couldn't kill anyone, whatever they might have done!"

"So where was he? Why did he need you to give him an alibi?"

Harriet buried her face in her hands and was silent for a moment, then she raised her head and said, "If I tell you, you must promise not to say anything to anyone."

"I don't know if I can promise that."

"I swear it had nothing to do with Gordon's death!"

"So tell me."

She looked down at her hands, now folded in

her lap. "He was at the shop—at least he was in the flat. With Wendy."

"With Wendy?"

"Yes, they've been seeing each other for a little while now. I know it's wrong—well, it was when she was Gordon's wife—but they love each other."

She looked at me almost defiantly and I said, "I understand."

"Do you? Do you see how I couldn't let anyone know, even after Gordon was dead. Roy . . ." Her voice trembled. "Roy would have been so angry."

"Yes, I can imagine. How long have they been seeing each other?"

"A couple of months, before Gordon died. Wendy was so unhappy—Gordon was playing around again—and Donald, well, he's always been fond of her. I suppose it just sort of happened. I pick Mandy up from the shop and take her out for a couple hours . . ."

She looked down again at the child asleep in her pushchair. "Donald's so fond of her, as if she was his own. Gordon," her voice hardened, "he never cared for her at all. She was the reason, you see, why he had to marry Wendy. He'd no intention at all of marrying her until she got pregnant and Roy made him, so he always resented poor little Mandy." She looked at me in silence for a moment, as if calculating my reaction to what she was about to say. "I know it's a wicked thing to say about your own son, but sometimes I'm *glad* Gordon's dead. He made so many people unhappy. Not just Wendy and Donald—he was always picking on him and making his life miserable, right from when they were tiny—but he was very unkind to me, always making sarcastic and cruel remarks, siding with Roy to put me down. Sometimes it seemed that he didn't really care for anybody. Oh, there were these women, but he never *loved* any of them, they were just conquests to him. He didn't believe any woman could resist him! That poor girl in the office, the one they arrested, I don't remember her name—he couldn't believe she wouldn't fall for him like all the rest. Well, he certainly got a surprise there when she stood up for herself!"

"Her name's Thea Wyatt," I said. "She's engaged to my son."

She put her hand over her mouth. "No! I'm so sorry, I didn't know . . ."

"They haven't announced it yet."

"The poor girl! Put in prison like that when she didn't do it."

"I gather that your husband still thinks she did."

"Oh, Roy! He has to have someone to blame, he's like that. Anything bad's always someone else's fault! But the police said they had evidence she didn't do it, isn't that right?"

"Yes, it is. No, Thea's been absolutely cleared. But, as you can imagine, it's left her in a pretty bad state. She's been very brave, gone back to work and everything, but she's not going to be right until the real murderer is caught."

Harriet looked at me curiously. "And that's why you were asking me those questions. You thought Donald had killed Gordon?"

"It seemed a possibility," I said. "From what you say, there was a motive."

"But you do believe me, don't you?" she asked urgently. "He and Wendy were at the flat. They had nothing to do with it."

"Yes, I believe you. And you were seen here by Chloe just about the time the murder was committed, so you have an alibi."

Her eyes widened. "You don't mean you thought *I* might have done it?"

"Well . . ."

"He was my son," she said in an agitated manner, "even though we didn't get on, and I did say I'm glad he's dead, but no, you can't believe I'd do *that*. No mother could!"

"No, of course I didn't seriously think so. It was just a question of alibis."

The formal phrase seemed to calm her and she reverted to her earlier theme.

"Wendy and Donald are so happy together, and now Gordon's dead there's no real reason they couldn't get married. But Roy would be terribly angry, he'd make all our lives a living hell!"

"It seems so unfair."

"Roy never was fair," she said bitterly.

"I suppose . . ." I hesitated. "I suppose you could go away—all three of you."

"Go away?" She looked stupefied. "We couldn't. Donald's business . . ."

"Yes, you could," I said, warming to my theme. "Donald's business is largely mail·order, isn't it? I mean, he could do it from anywhere. You could go far away—Scotland, perhaps, where Roy couldn't find you."

"If only we could . . ."

"Oh *do*," I cried. "You could all make a fresh start. No one would know you. Donald and Wendy could get married. It would be perfect!"

"Could we?"

"Look," I said, "I have no right to say any of this, but it seems to me that it wouldn't take more than one resolute act to make three people happy."

"They might not want me with them," Harriet said. "And I *couldn't* stay behind to face Roy after they'd gone!"

"They'd understand that. Anyway, I think Donald loves you very much, and Wendy, not to mention little Amanda."

Her face softened. "No, Mandy would miss me."

"They all would."

The child in the pushchair stirred and whimpered slightly as children do when they start to wake.

"We must be getting back," Harriet said, getting up from the seat and bending over to reassure her granddaughter.

"Ask Donald and Wendy what they think about moving," I said. "Don't tell them that it was my idea, though."

She straightened up with the first proper smile I'd ever seen her give. "Yes," she said, "I'll do that. I'll see what they think." She lowered her voice, as though she thought we might be overheard. "I've got a little money put away. It's in a post office account, so Roy doesn't know anything about it. It's not much, only a few thousand, but it would help to get us started, wouldn't it?"

"It certainly would."

She pulled up the hood of the pushchair and tucked the rug more firmly around the child.

"For Mandy's sake—they'll see it's the best thing."

"Well," I said, "good luck."

She put her hand on my arm. "I'll never forget your kindness," she said. "I'm really grateful."

"I hope it works out for you all," I said.

She waved, almost absently, as she moved away, her thoughts obviously busy with plans for the future.

"Oh, Ma!" Michael said, when I told him. "You interfering old busybody!"

"Nonsense," I said. "I prefer to think of myself as a sort of Flora Poste, tidying up people's lives and making them happy."

Though, in my heart, I did wonder if what I had done was the right thing after all.

Chapter Seventeen

"It's just occurred to me," I said to Michael at breakfast next morning. "I suppose I'd better let Roger know what's happening."

"Happening?" Michael said absently, scooping the last of the marmalade out of the jar.

"About Donald Masefield and the others. I mean, if they all three suddenly up and leave, he's going to draw the wrong conclusions, isn't he?"

"Yes, you had better. I don't envy you, though."

"What do you mean?"

"Having to confess you've been withholding evidence."

"Oh, nonsense! Well, I know I didn't exactly tell him immediately about Harriet's alibi being false— and, mind you, it was Jilly, his own wife, who told me about that—but if I had he'd have confronted her and I bet she wouldn't have told *him* about Donald and Wendy!" Nevertheless it was with some trepidation that I did eventually get hold of Roger and told him all about my meeting with Harriet.

"I'm sorry I didn't tell you about Harriet straightaway. But," I added placatingly, "I did get it all out of her in the end."

Roger laughed. "I suppose I must reconcile myself to your own peculiar methods, unorthodox though they may be. And, yes, you probably got to the bottom of it more easily than I would have done. But *please*, Sheila, if you do get any other little bits of information like that, could you tell me and let *me* decide how they should be interpreted?"

"Yes, Roger," I said docilely, "of course I will."

"I wish I could believe that. But well done, anyway. At least we've eliminated that lot."

"Which leaves us with what?"

He sighed. "I wish I knew. We're really not making much sense of any of it. I've taken away a lot of papers from the office, in case anyone was up to something and Gordon Masefield was blackmailing them. That seems to be the best so far. I must get down to sorting them out."

"Actually," I said hesitantly, "there is one other thing I didn't tell you."

"What is it?" Roger asked resignedly.

"Someone saw Gordon Masefield and Jason Chapman's wife, Laura, having lunch together in Taunton a little while before he was killed."

"So? It might have been perfectly innocent, some sort of business thing."

"No, I don't think so. Miriam Yates—that's the person who saw them—said, and I quote, 'They were all over each other,' and they were in a wine bar, tucked away at the other end of Taunton, where they wouldn't expect to see anyone they knew."

"Except your friend Miriam Yates. Is she really sure it was him?"

"Oh, yes. Her daughter Karen used to go out with him at one time and Miriam never liked him. No, she went up and spoke to him. She said he was *very* embarrassed."

"I should think he would be!"

"So you see, if Jason Chapman knew that his wife was having an affair with Gordon Masefield, then he had a perfectly good motive for killing him."

"I agree that he had a motive. Unfortunately he also has an unshakable alibi. He was at the dentist. At precisely the time Gordon Masefield was murdered, Jason Chapman was having a highly expensive crown fitted."

"Oh, bother!"

"Exactly."

"Oh well, back to the drawing board."

"Yes, well, you will remember what I said about sharing information, won't you?"

"Of *course*, Roger," I said meekly. "Give my love to Jilly and the children."

"Roger was a bit miffed with me," I said to Rosemary when she came round for coffee later. "Though, I must say, I can't altogether blame him." And I told her all about Harriet and Donald and Wendy.

"No! Really! What an extraordinary thing!"

"You mustn't tell anyone," I said. "If they *do* make a bolt for it, no one must know in case Roy Masefield tries to find them."

"I wouldn't dream of it," Rosemary assured me. "But fancy little mousy Harriet doing such a thing—and little mousy Wendy, too, come to think of it. You must have been very persuasive!"

"I did my best. I really couldn't bear to see all three of them—four with the little girl—leading such miserable lives just for the want of a little push."

"Do you think they will?"

"I think there's a pretty fair chance. Donald's pretty determined under that mild exterior. I mean, look how he stuck to his guns about having the bookshop. That can't have been easy with his father ranting and roaring at him!"

"No, you're right. I wonder why they didn't think of it themselves, though?"

"Oh, you know how it is when you're sort of locked into a situation, you never look further than the problem itself! It's always easier for an outsider to see a solution."

"I suppose it is. Well, good luck to them! I jolly well hope they make it."

"Oh, so do I!"

"And, in any case," Rosemary said, returning to my original remark, "I don't think Roger has any right to be miffed with you. After all, you have eliminated a couple of suspects for him—saved him a lot of work!"

"I think he would have preferred me to go

through the correct channels, though he did admit that I'd probably done him a favor."

"Oh, talking of favors, could you do an enormous one for me?"

"Sure. What is it?"

"Could you return a book that my mother borrowed to old Walter Meredith?"

"Yes, of course . . ."

"I hate to bother you, but I really *can't* go and see him!"

"Whyever not?"

"Well, you know he's a great chum of my mother's and he seems to think it would please her if he invited Jack and me to Sunday lunch. He's asked us several times and I really can't go on making excuses!"

"Would it be such a dire thing to have to do?"

"A bit tedious. No, it's not that. I wouldn't mind going, but Jack simply refuses."

"Oh dear."

"Partly because he absolutely *hates* having Sunday lunch anywhere except in his own home, and partly because he can't stand poor old Walter—he says he's like the worse kind of maiden aunt!"

"I suppose he is a bit. Actually, now I come to think of it, he's *very* like Georgie in the Lucia books, always dusting his bibelots!"

"Exactly. So would you be an angel? I'll drop the book off on my way back from Mother's just before lunch."

*   *   *

With the book (a life of the Queen Mother) in my shopping bag, together with a pot of lemon marmalade as a sort of offering, I arrived on the doorstep of Walter's cottage down by the harbor just as his daily, Mrs. Yalding, was on the point of leaving. She put her head round the door and called out loudly, "You've got a visitor, Mr. Meredith!" Turning to me, she said, "You have to shout a bit now, Mrs. Malory, he doesn't hear so well as he did and he forgets to put his hearing aid in." She put her carrier bag onto the handles of her bicycle, gave me a cheery wave, and pedaled away.

Walter came bustling out to greet me.

"Sheila! Come in, come in. What a lovely surprise!"

He ushered me into the sitting room and I was struck once again, as I always was, at the number of objects he had managed to cram into a relatively small space. The walls are so covered in pictures that it's impossible to see more than a few square inches of wallpaper. There are shelves and cabinets stuffed full of pieces of silver and porcelain and there are also numerous footstools, covered with tapestry work (another of Walter's passions) which make navigating the remaining floor space a hazardous business. To be fair, Walter has a very good eye for an antique and most of the things on display are of very high quality. The room itself is not large, with only one quite-small window, so that the general effect is claustrophobic, not to say overpowering.

I lowered myself gingerly onto an elegant but

fragile Regency sofa—rosewood with gilded sphinxes for feet—beautiful, but, as I remembered, hideously uncomfortable, and explained about returning the book and handed him the jar of marmalade, which he received with expressions of enthusiasm. We chatted for a while and I was saddened to see that he, like so many of my mother's generation, had become frailer and more abstracted, sometimes not really taking in what I was saying, as if his mind was elsewhere.

"Wonderful woman, the Queen Mother," he said, not for the first time. "I met her once—did I tell you?—at one of the palace garden parties. She was wearing a lilac hat and frock, so elegant . . . Queen Mary was elegant, too—those beautiful ivory-handled parasols! I met *her* several times. There was a lady who knew about antiques! I remember her talking about a particular piece of porcelain she had, Meissen, a gift from Princess Alice of Hesse to her mother, Queen Mary's mother, that is . . ."

I shifted uncomfortably on the Regency sofa and tried to concentrate but the words flowed over me and I looked around the room again, admiring a fine pembroke table against one wall and a pair of Trafalgar chairs against another.

". . . So very sorry to hear that Lois Barber is so ill again." Walter was back in the present day once more.

"Yes," I said. "I'm afraid that cruise didn't really do her any good."

"Poor Hugh! Such devotion! And so dreadful for him to have had that unpleasantness just before he went away." Unpleasantness seemed an inadequate way of describing Gordon Masefield's murder. "That wretched young man," Walter continued. "Something of a ne'er-do-well, from what I hear."

"Not very nice, certainly," I said.

"And you know Hugh was here, with me, the very afternoon that it happened!"

Walter seemed quite animated at the thought of being connected, however remotely, with such a dramatic event.

"Really?"

"Oh yes. He came to bring me some papers to sign—a trust I've set up, you know. The police came round to check his—what do they call it? His *alibi*." He pronounced the unfamiliar word triumphantly. "And, of course, I was able to tell them that he was here at what I gather was the relevant time, four o'clock."

"Really?"

"Indeed. I was quite sure about it because Hugh and I were chatting and he looked up at that clock on the mantelpiece—yes, that one there, it's French, you know—and he said, 'Good heavens, is that the time? Four o'clock already!' So you see, there was no mistake about that!"

"No, indeed. It *is* a pretty clock."

I got up to have a closer look at it. It was pale blue enamel with filigree gold decorations and delicate gold hands.

"It is very fine, and an excellent timekeeper," Walter said. He got to his feet. "Now then, what about a cup of tea? Mrs. Yalding will have left a tray all ready."

"So there we are," I said to Michael. "Jason Chapman was at his dentist and Hugh was with Walter, Donald and Wendy were—how shall I put it?—otherwise occupied, and Harriet was feeding the ducks with her granddaughter. We seem to have run out of suspects."

"Yes," Michael said absently, "I suppose we have." He fitted the last pieces of pottery together and wound some cellotape around the mended vase. "There, we'll just let it set properly and it should be as good as new. At least, until the next time Foss knocks it off the mantelpiece."

"Oh, thank you, darling, that's splendid. I'm very fond of that vase, it was a wedding present from your Great Aunt Lydia. I don't know what I'll do about little jobs like that when you've gone!"

"I'm only moving a mile down the road! We'll still be in communication."

"Yes, I know, darling—silly of me."

Michael looked at me sharply. "You will be all right?" he asked. "I mean, you're not, as they say, losing a son, but gaining a daughter."

I laughed. "That's very true, and I'm so very fond of Thea. I've always longed for a daughter."

"Thank you very much!"

"You know what I mean. I'm really looking forward to that part of it. It's only—well, there's just been the two of us, ever since your father died, for so long . . . Oh, take no notice of me, I'm just getting maudlin!" I plugged the kettle in. "Tea or coffee?"

"Coffee, please."

"Anyway, as I was saying, there doesn't seem to be any suspects not accounted for."

"I suppose," Michael said thoughtfully, "there may have been people who hated Gordon Masefield's guts we simply don't know about."

"Quite likely, I should think. But would they have known where to get at him at work?"

"They might, if they were ex-clients."

"What do you mean?"

"Do you remember that divorce case that Jonah told us about—the one where Masefield practically destroyed the husband, who tried to commit suicide?"

"Oh, yes, I remember."

"Well, *he* would have had a pretty good motive, don't you think?"

"Well, yes, I suppose he would, but I still don't think he's a possible murderer. I mean, he certainly had the motive, but how about the means and opportunity?"

"But you must admit it's a possibility?"

"A remote one, yes. But a bit wild!"

I thought about Michael's wild theory, though, when I ran into Carol a few days later, when I was standing behind her in an interminable queue in the post office.

"Hello, Carol," I said. "How's Jackie?"

"Oh, hello, Mrs. Malory. She's okay. She's leaving, though."

"Really?"

"Yes, she said she really didn't fancy working in that place any more, she says it gives her the creeps. Well, you can understand that, can't you?"

"Yes, I suppose I can. So what's she going to do?"

"She's going to be a travel rep."

"Good gracious, that's a bit different from Barber and Freeman!"

"Well, she never really liked being in an office. It wasn't glamorous enough for her! No, she's just working her notice and then she's off. Between ourselves, Mrs. Malory, I think she just wants to put it all behind her, all that happened."

"I can imagine. Finding Gordon Masefield like that must have been really horrible for her."

"Oh yes, it was."

"Actually, Carol, there's something I meant to ask you. On that afternoon were there any clients in the office?"

She thought for a moment. "There was only one. Mr. Phillips came to see Miss Wyatt at two o'clock. He left at about half past. There wasn't anyone else. Well, Mr. Chapman and Mr. Barber were both out and Mr. Gascoigne was working on something complicated in his room and said he wasn't to be disturbed. No, there wasn't anyone else in the office. Oh, except the man about the photocopier."

"Who?"

"The man who came to fix the photocopier. It's really dreadful the way it's always going wrong!"

"When did he come?" I asked.

"About half past two, I think."

"And when did he leave?"

"I didn't see him go, but he wasn't there when I was making the tea at half past three, because I was going to offer him a cup."

I thought for a moment and then I said, "You say the photocopier's always going wrong. Was he the usual man who came to fix it?"

"Now you come to mention it, no, he wasn't. He said that Bill—that's the chap who usually comes—was on holiday. Why? Is it important?"

"I just wondered. Did you tell the police about him being there?"

"Well, no, I didn't. I didn't think, to tell you the truth. And, anyway, he must have gone long before anything happened."

"Yes, of course," I said reassuringly. "He probably didn't have anything to do with it." The queue moved forward. "Oh, look," I said, "it's your turn next."

When I got in I phoned Roger and told him what Carol had said.

"I don't suppose it's important. But it wasn't the usual man—it could have been anybody. And nobody saw him go. I mean, he could have been lurking in the gents' loo, biding his time."

"Certainly we must check him out. I can't say I'm very hopeful, though."

"Well," I said virtuously, "you did say to keep you up to date with any information I might find."

He laughed. "Very well. Point taken."

"Actually," I said, "photocopier repairmen are the sort of people you *expect* to find around an office, so obvious you don't notice them. Like—was it a postman?—in one of the Sherlock Holmes stories, or was it Father Brown?"

"Okay. Leave it with me. I'll let you know if anything comes of it."

"Well," I said, "it seems to me that we're running out of suspects, so a bit of new blood, as it were, wouldn't come amiss!"

Roger laughed again. "While you are around to find them for us, Sheila," he said, "I don't see us ever running short of suspects!"

Chapter Eighteen

Washing a reluctant dog is not an ideal way to spend a morning, but poor Tris was suffering from harvest mites between his toes and needed an antiseptic bath, so I put on an old skirt and blouse and enveloped myself in a large apron and braced myself for the task. Since he is a small dog I usually bath him in the kitchen sink and I'd just reached the stage of covering him with the evil-smelling shampoo that my vet assured me would do the trick, when the phone rang. I stripped off my rubber gloves and, entreating Tris to be a good dog and stand still, I went to answer it.

"Sheila?" It was Roger.

"Oh, Roger, can I call you back? I'm just in the middle of bathing the dog."

"Yes, all right. But there is something I feel I must tell you."

Roger's voice was grave and I was very tempted to ask him what it was all about, but a furious barking from the kitchen made me say hastily, "I've got to go now, but I'll ring you in half an hour."

All the time I was scrubbing away at Tris and

trying to hold him still while I was rinsing him, I wondered what it was that Roger had to tell me. Finally, after a tiresome session with the hair dryer, I settled the now unnaturally white dog in front of the sitting-room fire with a handful of biscuits and picked up the phone again.

"Roger, what news? Did you find out anything about the photocopier repairman?"

"Yes, I checked that with his firm. He was absolutely bona fide, and, anyway, he left before three and was busy repairing someone else's photocopier in Williton at the time of the murder."

"Oh, bother. So now we're left with no one!"

"Not exactly."

Something in Roger's voice made me pause.

"Roger, what is it?"

There was a moment's silence, as if Roger was considering how to put what he had to tell me.

"You know we took away some papers from Gordon Masefield's room?"

"Yes, you told me."

"They were on the floor, presumably swept off his desk when he slumped across it, when he was killed."

"Yes?"

"One of the papers seems to indicate"—Roger's voice was completely colorless—"that Mr. Gascoigne was in that room at around the time of the murder."

"Jonah! But that's ridiculous! He was in his own room with the door shut, working on some sort of tax thing."

"That is what he led us to believe."

"Led . . . Oh, come on, Roger, you can't think that Jonah . . . What is this paper, anyway?"

"I shouldn't be telling you this, but—well . . . It's an E-mail addressed to him from someone in London, timed at three forty, that's just before the murder was committed and well after the time that Mr. Gascoigne allegedly shut himself away in his room to work on his tax papers."

"There must be an explanation! What does Jonah say?"

"That is the problem. Mr. Gascoigne is in Spain."

"What!"

"Jason Chapman informs me that Mr. Gascoigne traveled to Spain two days ago on the firm's business—something to do with a property contract for a client that had to be sorted out with Spanish lawyers."

"Well, then!" There was silence once again. "Oh, come on, Roger, you surely don't think that Jonah's done a runner? Have you tried to contact him in Spain?"

"I telephoned the hotel he is staying in twice and both times I was told that he was not there."

"Well, I expect he was seeing the Spanish lawyers."

"At eleven thirty in the evening?"

"You think he isn't taking calls?"

"I really don't know what I think."

"Have you called at his home? What does Caroline have to say?"

"Yes, I did call, but his wife wasn't there. A

neighbor said that she'd gone to stay with her mother, but she didn't know the address."

"Yes, well, she probably would when Jonah's away. Her baby's due quite soon now . . . Oh, really, Roger! You surely don't think that she's gone off to Spain as well!"

"It's a possibility."

"No, it *isn't*," I said vehemently. "Roger, I know these people! Anyway, what possible motive could Jonah have for killing Gordon Masefield?"

"Blackmail, perhaps."

"You mean that Jonah might have been doing something criminal and Gordon Masefield found out? But Jonah simply *wouldn't* do anything like that. I've known him since he was a little boy—he and Michael grew up together. He's the most honest, straightforward person I know, and there's no way he could *kill* anyone!"

"People do strange things when they're under pressure."

"No, Roger," I said firmly. "I am quite positive Jonah had nothing to do with all this and that there is a reasonable explanation for everything."

"You may be right," Roger said. "But I must say I would feel happier if Mr. Gascoigne had a more persuasive alibi for the time of the murder. In light of what we've found, being in his room with the door shut isn't quite enough."

Michael was very indignant when I told him about Roger's call.

"That's absolutely ludicrous! Jonah, of all people!"

"I know, I tried to explain to him that Jonah's the *last* person . . . But, of course, his alibi is a bit vague."

"But surely, if he was guilty, he'd have jolly well made sure that he *did* have an absolutely watertight alibi!"

"You'd think so."

I got some potatoes out of the vegetable rack. "Are you going to be in to supper tonight?"

"No, I said I'd go and take a bit off Thea's dining room door—she's got a new carpet and the door doesn't shut properly. I expect we'll get takeout."

"Did Jonah say anything to you about going to Spain?" I asked.

"No, but I expect Thea will know all about it."

"I told you Roger suspected Caroline of having gone to join him there. As if she'd go flying off like that in her condition! I mean, the baby's practically due at any minute."

"I'm sure Thea will know all about the Spanish business," Michael said, scrabbling about in his toolbox. "Ma, have you seen that small plane of mine, the one with the bit broken off the handle? Oh no, it's all right, I've found it."

"I expect," I said thoughtfully, "that Roger thinks that when Jonah knew the police had those papers from Gordon's room, the game was up and he seized the opportunity of this thing in Spain to get out of the country while he could."

"Well, then," Michael said, closing the lid of his

toolbox with a snap, "he thought wrong, didn't he?"

"Yes, of course he did," I said stoutly. "It's absolute rubbish."

I was still up when Michael got back.

"Thea knew all about the Spanish thing," he said. "But she couldn't explain the E-mail. It really is mysterious. We'll just have to wait until Jonah gets back."

The next day I had to go round to the Red Cross committee rooms to help my friend Anthea count the money from the collecting tins. It's a job I particularly hate—I keep losing count and having to start all over again, and when I've finished my hands always smell of coppers for ages after, however much I wash them. Still, we finished at last and were having a well-earned cup of coffee when Anthea said, "Oh, bother! I said I'd take that walking frame round to old Mr. Newton—his daughter asked if we had one we could lend him—and I simply *must* be back home by twelve because I've got the television repairman coming."

"That's okay," I said. "I'll take it."

"Oh, bless you! That would be marvelous."

"No problem. You'd better go now, you don't want to miss him."

"I know. Ron's been suffering dreadful withdrawal symptoms, not being able to get the football! Now, do you know the address? It's fifty-three Tregareth Road."

When she had gone, I rinsed out the cups and

locked up. The walking frame was an awkward shape and wouldn't fit into the boot of my car, but eventually I managed to get it balanced on the back seat and set off. Tregareth Road is quite near the sea and consequently the larger detached houses at the top end have mostly been turned into guest houses or holiday flats. Further down the road the houses are smaller and terraced. Until recently a lot of them had bed-and-breakfast signs in the window, but since the complicated EC regulations most of them have given up—sad, really.

I rang the bell of number 53 but there was no answer. I tried again and banged the knocker quite hard. I was just about to give up and go away when a woman wheeling a shopping trolley stopped outside the gate.

"Do you want Mr. Newton, dear?" she asked.

"Yes. I've got a walking frame for him, from the Red Cross."

"Oh yes, Eileen said someone was bringing one."

"I don't seem to be able to make anyone hear."

"No, well, you wouldn't really. He has the telly on that loud and he's deaf to begin with!"

"Oh dear . . ."

"Never mind, dear. I've got a key. Eileen leaves one with me, just in case. I'll let you in."

"Thank you, that would be kind."

"I'm Iris, Iris Pugsley. Come on in while I find it." She opened her front door and we went in.

"I just want to put the frozen stuff into the fridge," she said. "Go on into the lounge, I won't be a minute."

I opened the door and stood on the threshold, absolutely amazed. The small sitting room was absolutely crammed with plaster ornaments. Every surface—mantelpiece, windowsills, shelves, bookcases—was full of them. There was every sort of animal (deer, bears, dogs, cats, ducks, elephants), there were small boys with braces, small girls with aprons full of flowers, as well as gnomes, trolls, dragons, castles, cottages—everything that the mind could think of had been reproduced in plaster. There were even two dog baskets, complete with blankets, in each of which were seated several plaster dogs.

I edged my way gingerly into the room and waited. Presently Iris came in.

"Sorry to keep you," she said.

I felt I had to make some sort of comment on the plethora of ornaments.

"What a remarkable collection," I said. "It must have taken you years to collect them!"

She laughed. "Oh, they're not mine," she said. "They're my Barry's. He makes them. He gets the kits and makes them."

"Good gracious."

"He got the first kit about a year ago, from one of those magazines, and he's been on the go with them ever since. That's my Barry all over," she said proudly. "Once he gets keen on something he's at it all the time. Before this it was those airplane kits—he used to have them strung all over his room, you couldn't get through the door for them!" She laughed. "Mind you," she said, "this lot takes a bit of dusting. But then, it's nice when your kids have a hobby—keeps them off the streets."

"Yes, it is."

"Right then, I've got the key."

I picked up the walking frame and followed her out.

She unlocked the front door of the Newton's house calling out loudly, "Fred, Fred! It's me, Iris, I've got a visitor for you!"

A blast of music and a loud voice generating cheer with an American accent indicated that Mr. Newton was, indeed, watching television. He was sitting in an armchair with a rug over his knees, though the room seemed to me to be stiflingly hot. He acknowledged our presence briefly by glancing in our direction, but then his eyes seemed drawn back irresistibly to the screen, where some sort of game show seemed to be in progress, the competitors being egged on by the presenter, a small man with a lot of blond hair and an electric blue jacket, and by the audience, apparently in a state of advanced hysteria. Mrs. Pugsley went over and switched off the set.

"This lady's brought your new walking frame, wasn't that kind of her!" she spoke very loudly, almost in his ear. She turned her head and said to me, "You have to shout, he doesn't hear very well."

I moved over. "Don't you remember me, Mr. Newton? It's Mrs. Malory."

His eyes lit up and he extended a shaky hand, which I grasped. "Very nice to see you. Very good of you to come. Eileen will be in soon. Give me my dinner. I don't get out much now. She'll be glad to see you. Always very good to Eileen, you and Mr. Malory were."

"There now, isn't that nice! He remembers you!" Mrs. Pugsley spoke with pride, as though Mr. Newton's feat of memory somehow reflected credit on her. "Well, I'll leave you to it, then. Like he said, Eileen'll be back soon—she tries to get back on Wednesdays and Fridays to give him his dinner. He has meals-on-wheels other days—they get the key from me."

Still talking, she left the room and I heard the front door slam behind her.

When she had gone Mr. Newton and I had a sort of conversation. That is, he said over and over again what a good girl Eileen was and I agreed with him. I was just deciding that I really would go when I heard the front door again and Eileen Newton came in. She stopped in the doorway and looked at me with some anxiety.

"Mrs. Malory," she stammered, "what's the matter? Why are you here?"

"It's all right, Eileen," I said reassuringly. "It's just that I was at the Red Cross rooms this morning and Anthea asked me if I'd bring your father his new walking frame."

"Oh," she said. "Oh, thank you, that was very good of you."

I could see that she was still upset for some reason, so I went on chatting while she recovered herself.

"Your next-door neighbor very kindly let me in

and your father and I have been having a little talk."

"That's nice. Will you excuse me, Mrs. Malory, while I give him his lunch."

"Yes, of course. I must be going, anyway."

"No." She spoke abruptly and I looked at her in some surprise. "No, please," she went on. "If you wouldn't mind . . ." She hesitated. "There's something I'd like to talk to you about. Please."

"Certainly."

"Thank you. I'll just get Father's food."

She went into the kitchen and quickly returned with a bowl of soup and some sandwiches on a tray. She put them on a small table in front of his chair. "There you are, Father. You get started on that and I'll bring your pudding in after." She turned to me. "Would you mind talking in the kitchen?"

"No, of course not." She switched the television back on and I followed her into what was quite a large kitchen for the size of the house. There was a pine table and four chairs and she pulled out one of the chairs and said, "Do sit down. Will you have a cup of tea or coffee? I'm making one for Father."

"Yes, please, whichever you're making."

I sat down at the table while she filled the kettle.

"What is it?" I asked curiously. "What do you want to talk about?"

"I really don't know how to tell you," she said, bending over to plug the kettle in, so that I could hardly hear her.

"Come along," I said bracingly, "it can't be that bad!"

She took a deep breath. "Oh yes it is, it's really awful." She was silent again and I tried once more.

"Just begin at the beginning," I said.

"The beginning? That was months ago."

"Yes?"

"We've been very busy at work and they've been giving me quite a lot of really complicated things to do. I was very pleased that they thought that highly of me." She paused and I smiled encouragingly. "Well, there was this probate, not a very big estate, but the beneficiary was a good client of ours. Mr. Gascoigne did a lot of commercial contracts for him. Well, I was working on this and it was really quite straightforward so I was feeling quite pleased with myself. The beneficiary was going to sell the house and he'd already taken the items that he wanted, so I just went round to check that everything was all right before a firm came in to do the house clearance. The trouble is, I was in a bit of a rush that day. It was a Friday and I had to get back to give Father his lunch. Anyway, I went through the house quite quickly and everything seemed all right so I gave the firm the go-ahead and they cleared the house."

The kettle made a hissing noise and she switched it off and poured the water into the teapot.

"As I say, it was all quite straightforward and I forgot all about it. That is, until I had a phone call. It was the beneficiary, wanting to speak to Mr. Gascoigne. Well, he was out of the office that day, so

Sally put the call through to me." She put a large tea cozy carefully over the pot and looked up at me. "Oh, Mrs. Malory, he was *so* angry!"

"Angry? Why?"

"I'd done something awful. He'd left a box on the table in the hall—right where I should have seen it, if I'd been concentrating properly on what I was doing—with a note on it saying that it was to be taken away and kept in a safe place until he could collect it. But I *didn't* see it and so it was taken away with the rest of the stuff."

"What was in the box? Money, valuables?"

"Oh, no—much worse than that! Quite irreplaceable! It was the family's photographs, going right back to before the First World War!"

"Oh dear."

"Yes, well, you can imagine how I felt! I rang the firm who'd cleared the house, of course, and they were very sympathetic, but the note must have got lost when everything was being moved, so they just thought it was all junk and to be thrown away."

"So what did you do?"

"I was really worried I'd get the sack. I mean, it's just the sort of thing that will lose you a client—well, you can understand why I sent an E-mail (the client was in America) saying we'd be looking into the matter and—well, I signed it with Mr. Gascoigne's name. You see, I thought if I did that I might be able to cover it up."

"Not a good idea," I said.

"No. Especially since Mr. Masefield somehow

managed to discover what I'd done—the original mistake and trying to cover it up. He was really horrible about it. He threatened to tell Mr. Chapman and have me dismissed. I pleaded with him and he said he'd consider it—he might want me to do something for him in exchange. He didn't say what, but *I* think he'd been doing something not quite right with one of the client's bills—he'd fixed the timing in some way—and he wanted *me* to cover up for *him*."

"What a horrible man he was!"

She nodded. "I was so scared. You see, Mrs. Malory, having this job means so much to me. Not just the extra money, though that does make such a difference, with Father the way he is, but to feel that I've really achieved something with my life! And if I was dismissed I'd never get another job like it."

"So what happened about Mr. Gascoigne's client?"

"Well, I E-mailed him the bad news and he was very annoyed and said that he expected a personal letter of apology."

"From Mr. Gascoigne?"

"Yes."

"What did you do?"

"I wrote a very long and apologetic letter and I took it in to Mr. Gascoigne, with some other letters to be signed, when I knew he was on the phone."

"And he signed it without looking?"

"Yes. He always did. He trusted me, you see, to have everything correct." She looked at me and shook her head. "I was so ashamed! To betray his trust like that!"

"Was that the end of it?"

"Oh, no, it gets even worse! You see on the day that Mr. Masefield died I went upstairs to the room where we keep the old files to put something away. I'd just received an E-mail from the client, accepting Mr. Gascoigne's apology but saying that he would be taking his business elsewhere when he returned to England, so I was a bit upset. I had the E-mail with me—I didn't dare leave it lying about—and I thought I'd just go and have a word with Mr. Masefield, to try and appeal to him once more." She paused for a moment, as if nerving herself to continue. "Well, his door was closed so I knocked. There was no reply so I opened the door and there he was! Lying there, dead! Oh, it was *horrible*! I didn't know what to do—I just panicked and ran away. Jackie and Carol weren't there—I don't know where they were—so no one saw me come downstairs. I just went into my office and sat there shaking! I didn't know what to do. I really don't know how long I sat there, but the next thing I knew there was all this uproar. Jackie had found him, so I didn't have to say anything, or explain why I'd been there."

"I see."

"It was only after a while that I realized that I must have dropped the E-mail in Mr. Masefield's office. There was no way I could get it back and then the police took things away . . . It was awful. I kept expecting someone to say something. But then

I heard, this week, that they think the E-mail means that Mr. Gascoigne was in Mr. Masefield's office round about when he was killed. They think he killed him!"

"When you were up there, before you went into Mr. Masefield's office, was Mr. Gascoigne's door shut?"

"Yes, just like he said—he was working on something and didn't want to be disturbed. His door was shut and Mr. Barber's was open, because he was out."

"And you didn't see anyone else up there?"

"Anyone else?" She looked puzzled. "No. There wouldn't be."

"No, I suppose not."

"So you see. It's awful. I've got to tell the police it was me—who dropped that E-mail, I mean—and then it will all come out. About the client, and deceiving Mr. Gascoigne, and not reporting the murder. They'll sack me for sure, and I don't know *what* the police will do."

She began to cry, dry, unaccustomed sobs. I went over and put my arm round her shoulder.

"It'll be all right," I said. "You never meant any of this to happen. Inspector Eliot is a friend of mine, he's a very sympathetic man. I'll come with you to see him. And Mr. Gascoigne is a really nice man, he'll be kind, I'm sure. Meanwhile, go and see Mr. Barber and tell him what you've told me. He knows what it's like to look after an invalid, I'm sure he'll understand."

"Do you think so?"

"I think he will. Anyway, you've got to tell him."

"Poor man, he's got trouble enough of his own. I heard his wife's really bad again. He's only in the office a few days a week now."

I took the cozy off the teapot. "Look," I said, "let's have a cup of tea and then we'll decide what to do first."

"Oh dear," she said, "it'll be stone cold! I'll make some more."

Chapter Nineteen

"There you are, then," Michael said when I told him about Eileen Newton. "The perfect motive. *And* she admits to being in Gordon Masefield's office more or less at the time of the murder."

"No way. There's no way Eileen would murder anybody!"

"Even if she was as desperate as she said she was?"

"Absolutely not," I said firmly. "It simply isn't in her nature, any more than it's in Jonah's."

"At least he's in the clear now."

"Yes, I went with Eileen to see Roger and she explained everything to him."

"What happened?"

"He gave her a bit of a ticking off about not telling the truth and withholding evidence and so forth, but she said he was very nice. So there we are."

"Well, *where* are we? It seems like a very dead dead-end."

"That's true," I said wearily. "If we accept that Jonah's telling the truth (which we do) and Eileen saw his door shut and Hugh's room empty and no one else around in the closed file room or anywhere—then I really don't see how the murder can have *happened*!"

"Well, we'll just have to leave it to Roger or Fate or something."

"I suppose so. But it really niggles away at me. I keep feeling that there's *something* we know that's the key to the whole thing, if only we knew what it was!"

"You're probably right, but let's drop it for this evening if Thea's coming. I think she really is beginning to put it behind her now . . ."

"Goodness! Is that the time? She'll be here in a minute—I must go and make the onion sauce. Will you be an angel and lay the table for me?"

I must say Thea did seem to be more her old self, and, although she didn't mention the office, she was lively and full of chat.

"Any date for the wedding yet?" Rosemary asked when I told her about our pleasant evening the next day.

"No, not yet. I don't think she's *that* ready to get on with her life. Anyway, there's plenty of time to think about it."

"Oh yes, talking of time, when are we supposed to be meeting for the Antiquarians do?"

"I think the coach leaves at six thirty. Is your mother coming?"

"Yes, worse luck. I told her that Wadeford Hall is practically at the other side of the county and that we wouldn't be home until after eleven, but it didn't put her off in the slightest. It did put Jack off though, so I'll have to drive us both. Are you going in the coach or will you come with us in the car?"

"Oh, come with you, please. They're stopping at The Royal Oak for supper on the way home and you know how people linger until closing time! If you're on the coach you have to stay till the bitter end."

"Well, I can't promise anything—you know what Mother's like when she's got the bit between her teeth—but I'll do my best!"

Looking round at the members, I thought what a lot had happened since the last Antiquarians' gathering. Hugh and Lois Barber weren't there, of course.

"She's much worse," Mrs. Dudley told me. "Day *and* night nurses. It can't be long now."

"Oh dear, poor Hugh."

"I can't see him carrying on when she goes. He'll be lost without her. Hugh Barber's been doing what Lois has told him since they were both in their twenties."

"Shouldn't she be in hospital?"

"Of course she should. But no, she refuses to go. Says she's going to die in her own bed."

"Yes, we all would, but it's not fair on poor Hugh."

"Lois Barber was born selfish," Mrs. Dudley said. "And," she went on, "selfishness is something I cannot abide."

I gulped slightly at this, since Mrs. Dudley could well have been the personification of Selfishness in a medieval morality play.

"It must be so distressing for Hugh to see her like that, he absolutely adores her."

"You mark my words. When she goes he won't last six months." With some difficulty she got up from the chair where she had been resting and leaned on her stick. "Sheila, perhaps you'd be good enough to give me your arm, since Rosemary seems to have disappeared. I want to see this famous porcelain they've been making such a fuss about."

When Mrs. Dudley had inspected (and dismissed) the porcelain and had been condescending about the tapestries, we caught up with the others in the Long Gallery.

"Oh, there you are, Mother!" Rosemary said with some asperity. "I've been looking everywhere for you!"

"If you *will* go rushing ahead like that." Mrs. Dudley was a past mistress of the art of counterattack. "I simply stopped for a word with Sheila. Now then, what else is there to see? I must say there hasn't been anything particularly worth seeing so far."

Actually there were quite a few things worth seeing and it was later than usual that we all gathered at The Royal Oak for our supper. It's a pleasant pub, one we often use on these expeditions, and the food is remarkably good. Rosemary and I were, of course, at the same table as Mrs. Dudley and, since it was a table for four, she summoned one of her cronies to fill the vacant seat. On this occasion it was Walter Meredith.

"How delightful," he said as he eased himself into the corner seat, "a table full of charming ladies! What could be more pleasant!"

"What are we having to eat?" Rosemary asked. "I'd better order it now, you know how long it always takes."

The menu was written up on a blackboard a little way away and Mrs. Dudley put on her spectacles to consider her choice.

"What on earth is Boudin of Pheasant?" she demanded.

"I think it's a sort of sausage filled with pheasant meat," I said.

"Why couldn't they say so? Ridiculous nonsense. I'll have the salmon with hollandaise sauce . . ."

"Oh, Mother, should you? It's rather rich for this time of night!"

"And," Mrs. Dudley continued implacably, "for pudding I'll have the creme brulee."

Rosemary sighed. "Yes, Mother. Sheila, what are you having?"

"I'll have the Boudin of Pheasant," I said defiantly, "and I don't think I can manage a pudding."

Rosemary gave me something resembling a wink. "Okay," she said. "And what about you, Walter?"

"Oh, I'll have the—what Sheila's having. I'm sure it will be excellent." He stood up. "Let me get everyone a drink. White wine all round as usual?"

He trotted off after Rosemary and Mrs. Dudley snorted. "He didn't want that pheasant thing," she said scornfully. "He only said he did because he couldn't see the menu and he's too vain to wear his glasses. Silly old fool!"

It was Mrs. Dudley's habit to describe as old people some years younger than herself, and, certainly, she did seem to have more life and energy than a lot of them.

Walter and Rosemary came back from the bar with the drinks and we settled down to a monologue from Mrs. Dudley about the shortcomings of the house we had just visited and the inefficiency of its owners. When she had exhausted that topic she began her usual quest for news and gossip.

"Well, Walter, what have you got to tell us?"

"Bob Richards has had another stroke, he's in Musgrove and so's Nora Blakely, she's got pneumonia. Andrew Roberts has had his bypass and he's back home now, but I don't think poor Phyllis is coping very well . . ."

The litany of illness continued and I withdrew my attention and addressed myself to my food, which had just arrived. I thought it was very good but I noticed that Walter didn't eat much of his. I don't know whether this was because he was too busy talking or if Mrs. Dudley was right and he'd only chosen the pheasant because I had.

"Oh, yes," he was saying, "and I had a letter from Esme Beresford. She's coming home shortly."

"Really?" I said. "I thought she was staying out there all winter."

"Apparently an old friend of hers is very ill and she wants to see her."

"An old friend?" Mrs. Dudley asked sharply. "Who is that?"

"Someone called Grace Compton," Walter said.

"Compton? I've never heard of her."

"She lived in Lichfield."

"Oh, *Lichfield.*" There was a wealth of contempt in Mrs. Dudley's voice. It was obvious that she couldn't be expected to know anyone who lived so far north.

"Will Mrs. Beresford be going back to Antibes?" I asked.

"Oh yes, I think so. This will just be a brief visit. A little while in Lichfield and a few days back here in Taviscombe to see to a couple of business matters."

"Absolutely ridiculous, gadding about the world at her age. You'd think she'd have more sense." Mrs. Dudley hated other people doing things that she did not, especially in faraway places beyond her jurisdiction.

"I wish I was in Antibes," I said. "I really dread the winter nowadays. I hate the cold and when the weather's bad the animals drive me mad when they can't go out!"

"You make a fool of yourself over those animals, Sheila," Mrs. Dudley said. "And as for the cold, well, your generation doesn't know what cold really is—all this central heating! When I was a girl there was one small coal fire in the drawing room and nothing else. We had a fire in the bedroom if

we were ill, but that was all. We wrapped up
warm, and it never did us any harm, did it, Walter?"

"Harm? No, of course not. Absolutely not!"

I thought of Walter's overheated cottage and
smiled.

"Are you going back in the coach, Walter?" Mrs.
Dudley asked.

"Well, yes, I expect so."

"You had far better come back by car with us.
I'm sure I saw that coach driver drinking something."

"It was only shandy, Mother," Rosemary
protested. "And he only had half a pint."

"That's still drink. Come along, then. I want to
get to my bed even if you people are prepared to
stay in this smoky atmosphere all night."

I don't know if it was the Boudin of Pheasant but
I had a restless night. It took me ages to get off and
when I did I had a strangely unpleasant dream, in
which Walter Meredith and Esme Beresford were
running along a promenade in the South of France,
both of them wearing Venetian carnival masks and
cloaks and shrieking with wild laughter as they
ran.

The next day Eileen Newton telephoned.

"I just want to say thank you, Mrs. Malory," she
said. "It was really good of you coming to the police station with me like that."

"Not at all. I was glad to do it."

"Like I told you, Inspector Eliot was really nice

about it. I know what I did was wrong—not reporting the death—but he was very understanding."

"What about Mr. Barber? Have you spoken to him?"

"Oh yes, I went to see him straightaway when I got back from the police station."

"So what did he say?"

"Well, he called in Mr. Gascoigne—he's back from Spain now—and I told them what I'd done. Everything. About the house clearance and the letters I wrote."

"And did you tell them about Gordon Masefield blackmailing you?"

"Oh yes, I told them absolutely everything."

"So what happened?"

"Well, they both gave me a real talking-to, but they said that, in view of my good record, they weren't going to do anything about it this time."

"Oh, I'm so glad."

"Actually, Mr. Barber was very sympathetic about Father and he said he understood why I was so worried about losing my job. Though, of course, he did say that it didn't excuse what I'd done, which it doesn't. And Mr. Gascoigne made me laugh!"

"Really?"

"He shouted a bit and then he said, 'Good God, woman! Am I such an ogre? We all make mistakes. For Heaven's sake come and *tell* me next time!' Well, I said I hoped there wouldn't be a next time and that was that. They were really nice."

"Yes, they're kind people."

"Anyway, I just wanted you to know what happened and to thank you for telling me what to do."

"Now you can stop worrying. You've got quite enough on your plate with your job and looking after your father."

"Oh, Iris is very good, she's a real friend. I'm very lucky, to have good friends and a good job."

"And do you know," I said to Michael, "I think she really does believe that! I'm so glad it's all sorted out so well. So how's Jonah? Did you see him last night at the cricket club meeting?"

"Yes, he's tickled to death to think that the police had him down as a murderer on the run in Spain!"

"So where was he when they rang?"

"The first time he was seeing the Spanish lawyer."

"But what about the eleven thirty call?"

"He was out having dinner with his client. You know how late they eat in Spain. Apparently no one ever goes out to dinner before ten o'clock!"

"I'm glad he was so kind to Eileen."

"Well, it wasn't the end of the world. The client they lost was going to South Africa, anyway, so he wouldn't have been bringing them much more business. Mind you, I think he'll read his letters a bit more carefully before he signs them from now on. I'm jolly sure I will!"

"Eileen's a good and conscientious worker, and I'm sure she'll never do anything like that again."

"All's well that ends well, then."

"Except, of course," I said, "it hasn't ended, has

it? The murder, I mean. We're as far away as ever from solving that."

"At least we know who it *wasn't*."

"That would be fine, if there was anyone left that it might have been. Even the photocopier repairman is in the clear."

"Well, it'll have to be Person or Persons Unknown," Michael said.

"Don't say that. I have this superstitious feeling that Thea won't name your wedding day until they've found the murderer."

"So you'd be stuck with me for ever. Yes, I can quite see why you want it cleared up!"

"Exactly," I said.

Chapter Twenty

I was just cooking the animals' chicken livers when the thought struck me. It was just a tiny thought to begin with, but when I went on from there it seemed to grow until it seemed a very big thought indeed. The trouble was it *was* only a thought. Still, I very much wanted to put it to the test, though I wasn't at all sure how to go about it. One thing I was sure of, though, I had to do this myself without bringing Roger into it. The spitting fat from the frying pan brought me back to reality and, while I wiped down the top of the cooker and put the livers in a bowl to cool, I decided to try the direct approach. So I rang up Barber and Freeman and made an appointment.

"Come in, Sheila," Hugh said, closing the door behind me and pulling out a chair for me. "What is it? How can I help you?"

I took a deep breath and began. "This is very difficult—I really don't know how to say this—but I must tell you that I am quite sure it was you who killed Gordon Masefield."

"My dear Sheila!" he said mildly. "What on earth are you talking about?"

"I don't have any proof," I said, "and you will probably deny everything, but I am absolutely sure of it."

"This is ridiculous!"

"It's your alibi, you see," I continued. "It worries me. You say you were at Walter Meredith's at four o'clock and that he confirms this. But when I was at Walter's and talked to him about it he was decidedly vague. He *is* vague now, and very suggestible. He told me *you* said it was four o'clock. He merely agreed with you."

"That's nonsense. He looked at the clock on the mantelpiece and confirmed that that was the time."

"Except that the clock in question has thin, delicate hands," I said. "It's very difficult to tell the time by it, especially if, like Walter, you're short-sighted and won't wear your glasses."

"But he told the police . . ."

"He's very vain—he wouldn't admit that he couldn't see for himself. I think you banked on that."

"But you're forgetting something," Hugh broke in. "I rang the office from there at four o'clock. Sally can confirm that!"

"No, you rang on your mobile phone; you just said you were with Walter. There was no reason for anyone to disbelieve you. You could have been anywhere."

"Sheila, look, I don't know why you're accusing

me in this way, with not a shred of proof, but I can assure you . . ."

"No," I said, "I know I have no proof, but I thought if I mentioned these things to Roger Eliot he might check your alibi a little more carefully than Inspector Bridges did."

Hugh was silent for a moment and then he said, "Why didn't you go to Roger Eliot straightaway? Why come to me?"

"Because I need to know. I need to know for Thea's sake. I thought you might tell me."

He laughed. "And you thought I might confess to murder!"

"I thought you might tell me the truth. You see, I think I know why you did it. Gordon Masefield was blackmailing you, wasn't he, like he blackmailed poor Eileen? I knew, when you were so sympathetic to her, that you understood only too well what sort of strain she was under."

"I was sorry for the woman, having to look after an invalid father . . ."

"Yes, that was something else you had in common," I said. "It was because of Lois, wasn't it? It was Lois's fault, really?"

"What do you mean?" Hugh burst out angrily. "What are you saying?"

"You needed money, a lot of money. I know you're not a poor man by any means, but Lois has always wanted a very rich lifestyle. And now, more than ever, she needed things, luxuries to make her life more bearable, flying on the Concorde, the glamorous cruise, and finally, all that expensive nursing care at home. Yes, you needed a great deal of money."

Hugh was silent so I went on, "I suppose you must have been milking—that's the term, isn't it?—the funds of one of your clients. I know it can be done."

Hugh sat very still, very quiet. Something suddenly occurred to me. "It was Mrs. Beresford's funds, wasn't it?" A fleeting expression crossed his face, so fast that I couldn't identify it.

"But she's coming home soon, isn't she?" I went on. "You're going to have to face the music soon, aren't you?"

I stopped and looked at him. His face was still impassive, but, as I looked, he suddenly buried it in his hands and I realized, with a mixture of surprise and horror, that he was crying. I didn't know what to do or say, so I simply sat there and waited to see what would happen next. After a few moments he raised his head, took a handkerchief from his pocket, and wiped his face. He seemed quite calm.

"You're right," he said. "It's only a matter of time now."

"Are you going to tell me what happened?" I asked.

"Yes. And in return I'm going to ask you a favor."

"But I don't think . . ."

"Hear me out," he said, "before you decide."

"Very well."

He put the handkerchief back in his pocket and leaned back in his chair.

"You are quite right," he said. "About the money, I mean. Have you any idea how expensive home nursing can be? Four hundred pounds a week for a day nurse, plus six hundred for a night nurse. And that's simply the basics. Medicines, specialist's fees—it's quite horrendous."

"Couldn't she have gone into a nursing home? I know they're expensive, too, but nothing like that."

"No," he said flatly. "She would hate that."

"But it's not fair to you!"

"I love her, Sheila. I want her to have whatever she needs—especially now. No. It was quite easy, really, especially when Esme Beresford was away. The trouble was it was too easy—I became careless and Gordon Masefield found out."

"And blackmailed you for money?"

"Oh, no. He wanted more than that. He wanted to become a partner. That wasn't so easy. Jason wasn't convinced that it would be a good idea and the longer it took the more impatient Masefield became and"—his face darkened—"the more arrogant. I really hated him, but I simply couldn't see any way out of it except to do what he wanted. He was becoming more and more importunate and dropping veiled remarks to other members of the staff. I felt I couldn't trust him to keep quiet. He was enjoying making me suffer—that's the sort of person he was. Then, that day, I had a chance to break free and I took it." He leaned forward as if to convince me. "You must believe me, Sheila, it wasn't premeditated—I simply saw a chance and I took it. Everything followed on from there."

He broke off and sat for a moment apparently lost in thought. Then he began again. "I was working in my room when I heard a sudden commotion. I went to the door and saw Thea coming out of Masefield's room and rushing down the stairs. I didn't think anything of it at the time—I just thought she was late for an appointment or something—so I went back into my room and went on working. But I kept turning over and over all that business with Masefield. I was half out of my mind with worrying about what would happen if they found out about Esme Beresford's money. Eventually, I thought I'd go and speak to Masefield, have it out with him somehow—I don't know what!" He gave a little laugh. "As you can imagine, I wasn't thinking very rationally. Anyway, I went into his room and found him sitting at his desk with blood on his face and papers all over the floor. I asked him what had happened and he started swearing and calling Thea every sort of filthy name. And then he started on me—threats and innuendos—I couldn't bear it any more. I just wanted to shut him up! I picked up that heavy lamp from his desk and hit him with it hard. Then he was quiet and I knew I'd killed him, that I was free of him. I stood there for what seemed a long time waiting for someone to come. I thought Thea would have said something—I couldn't understand why nobody came."

"Thea was very upset," I said. "She didn't tell

anyone what had happened, she simply ran out of the building and came to see me."

He nodded. "I realized that I was lucky. No one came from downstairs and Jonah's door was shut and he'd obviously heard nothing. Suddenly a plan simply dropped into my head and I knew what I had to do. I closed Masefield's door and went back into my room. I looked at my watch. It was three forty. I'd forgotten that I had an appointment with Walter Meredith at three forty-five, but I saw how I could turn it to my advantage. I knew, as you said, that Walter has become very vague and I thought I might be able to manage somehow to maneuver him into giving me an alibi. All I had to do was lie low for a little while and then ring (on my mobile as you guessed) as if from Walter's to ask for some papers from Masefield's room so that they would find the body when everyone thought I was out of the office. Then, in the confusion, I could slip out, coming back later having established my alibi."

"You were taking a lot of chances!" I said. "All sorts of things could have gone wrong."

"I thought they had when Eileen Newton suddenly appeared and went into Masefield's room. I was sure she'd raise the alarm and ruin my plan. But, to my astonishment, she just ran out, shutting the door behind her, and went away. And there was no outcry, nothing. I couldn't believe my luck." He was staring past me now, as if seeing in his mind once more the events of the day. "I was doing it all in a sort of dream," he said, "I can't explain. Somehow everything worked out. I made the phone call. Jackie found the body and while they were fussing around I slipped down the stairs and got out without anyone seeing me. When I got to Walter's I had another stroke of luck. He'd been dozing in his chair and when I arrived he had no idea *what* time it was, so I was able to convince him that I'd been there from before three forty-five until well after four. When I left I think he went to sleep again, so he wouldn't have realized that it was actually later than he thought. Then I went back to the office and made very sure that people saw me. You see, if people see you come in, they automatically assume they saw you go out."

"Yes," I said, "I suppose they do. Actually, there's one thing I don't understand. Where were you, before you went out? Eileen said your door was open and your room was empty. And she went into the closed file room as well, so you can't have been hiding there."

Hugh got up and went over to the large bay window behind him. He drew one of the long, heavy curtains slightly across the window.

"Simple," he said. "Just like in all the farces."

"But wouldn't you be seen from outside?" I asked, remembering how Rosemary and I had seen him from Park Street below.

"People very rarely look up, but in any case the windows have shutters, as you see." He drew the curtain back. "And if I unfold them just a little bit then I am screened from the road."

"I see."

In his eagerness to explain his cleverness Hugh

seemed to have forgotten the dreadful reason for it all.

"When I got back the police were here and Inspector Bridges . . ." His voice faltered.

"Yes," I said grimly. "Inspector Bridges went out and arrested Thea."

He was silent and I burst out, "Hugh, how *could* you? How could you let Thea go through an ordeal like that!"

He shook his head. "I know. I'm sorry. I felt terrible about it, but what could I do? If I'd confessed, what would have become of Lois? I couldn't do that to her!"

"So if Michael and Jonah hadn't discovered that Thea had an alibi you'd have let her rot in prison for the best years of her life!"

"No! I wouldn't have done that. When—when Lois—when Lois died, when she didn't need me any more, I was going to give myself up. I swear!"

"And you think that would have made everything all right?" I cried angrily. "You didn't see what it did to that poor girl, that terrible time in prison—what it's still doing! Don't you realize that this is why I've been so desperate to find out who the real murderer is, so that that shadow can be lifted from her life, hers and Michael's."

"I'm sorry, Sheila, I'm sorry . . ."

I was so angry, my heart was beating violently. For a while there was complete silence in the room. Vaguely I could hear the sounds of the traffic below.

"Esme Beresford will be back very soon now,"

Hugh said. "The doctors have given Lois just a few weeks. I pray that she will have gone before . . ." His voice broke.

My anger died down and I heard myself saying in almost friendly tones, "I find it really hard to think of you cheating an old woman like that. You've always seemed to me such an honest, generous man. You would have been the last person even to *think* of such a thing!" Suddenly I remembered something Mrs. Dudley had said. And I turned and looked at him sharply.

"But *you* didn't think of it, did you? It was Lois's idea, wasn't it?" He looked at me appealingly. "No, it's all right, you don't have to say anything. Mrs. Dudley said that you've always done what Lois told you, all your life, and this was just one more thing she told you to do. And what about Mrs. Beresford, was she to be made poor just so that Lois could have the luxuries of life?"

"Esme's a very rich woman indeed, even with what I've taken. And she had no one to leave it to."

"I don't think that's a real excuse, do you? No, I'm sure *you* didn't argue like that. It was Lois's idea, and Lois's argument."

"I love her so much." His voice was hopeless and there were tears in his eyes. "I love her so much and she's going to die."

He suddenly brought his fists down on the table and almost shouted, "Sheila, *please*, you've got to promise me you won't tell the police. Not yet. The moment it's all over, then I swear I'll give myself up, admit to the fraud and the murder. But you do see how I can't leave her now, at the very end, when she needs me as she's never needed me before!"

My head was whirling. I couldn't think straight.

"Please, Sheila, I *beg* you! If you've ever loved anyone in your life! Do this one thing for me—for Lois. I've told you it will all be over in a couple of weeks, perhaps less . . ."

I made up my mind.

"I'm not the person you should be asking, Hugh," I said.

He looked at me in bewilderment.

"What do you mean? Does anyone else know?"

"No, not yet. What I mean is—the person you must ask is Thea."

"Thea?"

"It seems to me that, after what you did to her, she is the one person who can give you what you want. Do you understand?"

He nodded slowly. "Yes," he said. "You're right. Please tell her what happened. Tell her that I am so very sorry for what I did to her, and beg her to give me this little space."

"Very well," I said. "I'll do that."

I got up to go. My legs felt weak and I was trembling. As I got to the door Hugh spoke.

"Sheila, explain to her how it is."

"I will," I said and went out closing the door gently behind me.

"So you see," I said to Thea, "that's how it happened and that is what Hugh is asking you to do."

"How could he do such a thing!" Thea cried. "How could he let me take the blame like that!" There were tears of anger in her eyes. "And then expect me to say nothing!"

The kitten, who had been playing with a ball of silver paper, looked up anxiously at the unaccustomed anger in her voice. I picked it up and put it on my lap.

"It is a great deal to ask of anyone," I said. "Especially someone who's had to go through what you did."

She went over to the window and stood for a while staring out at the sea, while I sat silently, stroking the kitten's soft fur. Then she turned and stood beside me.

"What do you think? What should I do, Sheila?"

I shook my head. "I can't make up your mind for you," I said. "You must decide, that's only fair."

"I can see *why* he did it, of course. But what he did—even leaving aside what he did to me—what he did was wrong."

"Yes, it was."

"He cheated Mrs. Beresford and he murdered Gordon Masefield. Nothing can excuse that."

"No. I don't think he is offering excuses, or even asking for forgiveness. What he is asking for is understanding."

"Do I understand," Thea said, "what it is to love someone so much that you're prepared to do that for them?"

"It's partly that," I answered. "But you mustn't forget that it was Lois who put him up to it in the first place. She is as responsible as he is. And, although Hugh would never admit it, I'm quite sure she knew that he murdered Gordon Masefield. That wouldn't have bothered her in the least, except for the possibility that he might be found out."

"What a loathsome woman!"

"I've never liked her, but the fact remains, Hugh has always been completely devoted to her, she has ruled his life. When she dies he will be utterly lost."

"And the doctors have only given her a few weeks?"

"Yes."

Thea threw up her hands in despair.

"How can I do it, then? If I told the police and Hugh was arrested, then it would all be for nothing, wouldn't it?"

"I suppose it would."

"So that's the answer then."

"Are you sure?"

She nodded. "Quite sure. I'll leave it to you to tell Hugh I won't say anything—I don't think I want to speak to him myself. Will you do that for me?"

"Yes, of course I will."

The kitten rolled over and began to kick my hand with its back feet, so I put it gently down.

"When Lois dies, he will tell the police what happened," I said. "But I don't think he will go to prison."

"What do you mean?"

"I mean that when Lois has gone he won't have any reason for going on living."

"No," Thea said quietly, "I don't suppose he will."

"It's strange, isn't it," I said, "how something as intrinsically good as love can, if it's excessive, or the wrong sort of love, turn into a kind of evil. Poor Hugh. I suppose, in spite of everything, we must pity him."

The kitten, bored with our lack of attention, began to sharpen its claws on the sofa, looking over its shoulder as it did so to make sure that we were watching. Thea laughed and picked it up.

"Little monster!" she said lovingly. Then, turning to me, she said, "Sheila, do you feel like coming shopping on Saturday? I thought we might start looking for my wedding dress. I believe there's quite a good place in Taunton and, if not, we can try Exeter or Bath. What do you say?"

I smiled happily. "That would be lovely," I said.